ill met by a fish shop on george street

Just when Jack Partridge had begun to think he was free of the past, strolling down George Street one spring afternoon, he suddenly came face to face with the one man in the world who could shatter that dream forever. The instant their eyes met, all his hopes of escape were stifled. A new life in another country and thirty years of respectability vanished in a trice. It was useless to run any farther. The flicker of recognition in that accusing glance convinced him that at last he must settle accounts. And the payment so long overdue was for murder . . .

As he has demonstrated in earlier mystery novels, Mark McShane once more proves his gift for summoning an incomparable blend of suspense, humor, and the heart-stopping twist of a surprise ending. His touch is deft, his ear attuned, and his eye camera-quick to catch the candid pose of crime.

SCENE: *Australia*

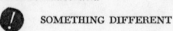 SOMETHING DIFFERENT

ill met
by
a fish shop
on
george street

MARK McSHANE

PUBLISHED FOR THE CRIME CLUB BY
DOUBLEDAY & COMPANY, INC.
GARDEN CITY, NEW YORK
1968

Library of Congress Catalog Card Number 68–10676
Copyright © 1968 by Mark McShane
All Rights Reserved
Printed in the United States of America
First Edition

ill met by a fish shop on george street

1

George Street, Sydney, is the Australian equivalent of Oxford Street and Fifth Avenue; or so they say in Sydney. Melbourne and Adelaide say otherwise. London and New York say nothing—they have never heard of George Street.

The truth is that if you ignore the architecture, mostly modern bottoms to bulky Victorians, like new trick feet on old dogs, this main shopping thoroughfare is like that of any other metropolis: fast-moving, loud, both brash and sophisticated, impersonal. Despite the notion that Australians are becoming more like Americans every day, the only resemblance here to New York, and a New York of fifty years ago at that, lies in the heavy sprinkling of obvious immigrants, or, as they are referred to generally, New Australians, which sounds a little politer if a great deal sillier.

Unusually, people on this particular afternoon were strolling, slowed from their city haste by spring weather lacking the humidity which would have driven them from one air-conditioned indoors to another.

Strolling at a slower pace than anyone else because he had more time to waste than anyone else, was Tom Brady.

He walked in a sloop, a sloping droop, head forward and shoulders rounded, belly out, flabby hands in a loose clasp behind, feet sauntering stiffly forward like those of a penguin and landing as flat as slapped-down books.

A large man, Tom Brady, ten pounds away from being fat, sixty years of such largeness responsible for his postural sag. Even if it had owned buttons his tweed jacket would not have been buttonable at the front, where a dark green sweater was stretched to pale green against its white background of shirt. His flannels had long since been kneed out of shape, his heavy boots could have done with a polish and the muffler which circled his neck was tinged with grease.

The over-all impression, a retired workingman without a wife, was true.

Not so true the impression given by his face. Tom Brady was no tough, in spite of the flattened nose (a football accident), the square jaw, the broad flat upper lip of a boxer (an Irish legacy) and the scar that ran through one eyebrow (poor judgement during the presentation of arms as a raw private)—these aided in their conspiracy by a bullet head butting almost neckless from broad shoulders and topped by short white curls.

It was a pale face, no hint of rude health or sun on the sagging features as flat and damp looking as poured porridge. Pale too the grey eyes and pale on expressiveness the mouth, which however had small chance to be anything other than an upcurving line under that bully of a lip. Only strong emotion disarranged his features. The interim barometer was his hands.

Held behind now as he slooped along George Street, his hands jiggled gently, the fingers going tap, flick and click against one another. As some people hum, Tom Brady played tunes with his fingers.

He was playing a tune to match his pace, leisurely, free of care. He had all the time in the world.

10

Tom's last job had ended five months before when he had been discovered asleep, which is not the sort of thing expected of a nightwatchman. He found, after spending the whole of one morning enquiring, that at sixty years of age it was not easy to get a job, people didn't want you, you were too old. He had given up the search, limiting himself to porings over the jobs-vacant columns of newspapers. This in time he also gave up. He had retired. He had become expert at doing nothing. Yet not for a moment would he have admitted that he was content. Constantly he reminded himself that he should look depressed, a ploy as useless as telling someone not to put his tongue in his mouth.

Tom was musing that what made up a bit for the misery of being jobless was the fact that downtown Sydney had tons of interest. There were always things to do or see. Most shop windows changed displays every week. The traffic was so dense it was a rare day that didn't produce a skirmish or minor accident, and the latter was good for at least an hour's watching. There were the big stores to walk around, people to look at, the post office steps to sit on, magazines to be found in waste-paper baskets, exhibitions where they gave away samples and tidbits and cups of coffee if you were careful not to look too interested, buildings being torn down or put up and a thousand other things. Sitting in the parlour at the boarding house was not bad, but George Street was better.

The people in front of Tom Brady were streaming into the open doorway of a department store. He followed. His shoulders gave a comfortable shrugdown and his fingers played a tiddly-om-pom-pom.

He passed Cosmetics, exchanged nods of familiarity with the woman on Combs & Brushes, cleared his throat past

11

Foundation Garments and turned into another aisle at the corner of Stockings, when he saw the demonstrator.

A small creased man inside a starched coverall, the demonstrator stood behind a trestle table on which were spread vegetables peeled, unpeeled and partpeeled around the stack of Miracle Peelers. He was talking hoarsely to no one, like a feeble father admonishing his children.

Tom Brady stopped, fronting the table. He would help by starting a crowd; and besides, demonstrators were entertaining, some good enough to be on the stage. One, with a sock-mender, he had listened to twice a day, morning and afternoon, for five days. Better than television, he had been.

The peeler man became more animated. He rasped to Tom and the surrounding air while producing wriggly tapeworms from potatoes and beets. Tom smiled at the jokes, nodded at the logic and shook his head defensively when told not to be skeptical or dubious.

At last, his audience remaining one, the demonstrator ran down in mid-spiel, not closing in for the sell because he no doubt knew from experience that Tom was a professional browser, not a buyer.

He smiled sadly at Tom, who said, "She's a bit slow today, eh?"

The man responded to the sympathy in Tom's voice. They talked, exchanging cigarettes—fortunately the same cheap brand—and reminiscences of the better days they had seen. When the demonstrator mentioned the high point of his career, an appearance at the Seattle World's Fair, Tom saw that the moment had come when he could bring out casually that he was retired from the police force. As usual, as expected, the recipient of this information became a shade deferential in manner, and Tom felt the usual warmth in-

12

side. He changed the subject. There was no need to go into details. "Retired from the police force" was enough.

Two women paused at the table. The demonstrator smothered them with hoarse words and began to make tapeworms. After a minute, with a conspiratorial nod at his new friend, Tom walked on, still glowing with his warmth.

He browsed for half an hour, on ground floor and basement. He would have gone upstairs also except for that escalator being out of order and he told himself he'd be buggered if he was going to climb steps, even though it did mean missing out the fun of Pets' Corner.

Passing swing doors in the basement he was brought to a worried halt by a sign. His hands separated, came to the front, tiptoed up his lapels, dithered on his chin and muffler.

The sign said: *Man wanted in Packing Room. Easy work. No skill needed.*

Taking a step to the side, Tom thought that really there was no sense in wasting time asking about the job. They would only say too old, much too old. Why should he allow himself to be snubbed?

He turned away, slooped at a risen pace up to the ground floor and out to the street.

This thing of employment, of losing a job and failure after long searching to find another, or of being in a job and stagnating, Tom Brady considered the story of his life. It had always been the same. As a youth, in England, his first job after leaving the Devonshire orphanage had been as a farm labourer, three months of which was enough to convince him he would never get anywhere working on the land. He became a navvy. Same thing. A truck driver. Same thing. A coal carrier, a scrap loader, a railway porter. Same, same, same. Two and a half years as a gardener brought only a ten shilling rise in wages. He went to London, where, following a series of short jobs to support a year of night school, he got himself on the police force. But although he worked hard for four years, somehow or another circumstances kept him a lowly beat constable. In the War it had been, Tom felt, a case of jealousy which had prevented a climb in the ranks from private. Even his wound hadn't earned him a medal, only a small pension.

As he thought of his wound, Tom began unconsciously and briefly to limp on his right leg, which however, apart from an ugly weal of scar tissue on the shin, was perfectly sound.

After demobilization, with a grateful government's lump sum and new suit, both soon to be shabby, he had looked around for something to do. While there was work aplenty, nothing appealed.

Britain's post-war austerity and drabness had helped in his seduction by advertizements that offered assisted passages to a land of perpetual sunshine and unlimited opportunity. A promise essentially kept, Tom found. There were not too many sunless days in a Sydney winter and whenever he lost a job he soon found another; and lost it and found another; and lost . . .

Meantime, love came into the life of Tom Brady. Or at any rate, during a period of indigence wherein he was unable to make his fortnightly visit to a King's Cross prostitute, he met a girl from Brisbane who was game for anything, even marriage. They married and lived rather drearily in small furnished flats. The children which might have held them together did not come. They drifted apart without rancour, she returning to Brisbane, living with another man and bearing three children, of the last of which she died. The whole marital episode concerned Tom less than a change in jobs.

14

And the jobs went on changing.

A watchman he came to be. Watching the night gloom pass through the warehouse windows, tapping his fingers, suffering that special placid boredom of the unimaginative, a boredom which stiffens not a resolve to work at something else but to remember, when there was no desire for dozing, to bring a comic or a newspaper or even a book. Tom thought it a pretty good job, all things considered.

Until he was caught asleep. Which, he sneak suspected, had been arranged. Someone had slipped a pill into his flask of cocoa and then telephoned the boss to come around and check. Why? Well, obviously the someone wanted to get a relative into the job.

It had always been the same. They had always been against him.

Tom shook his head, which had started to pain slightly, as it generally did whenever he indulged in prolonged thought.

However: he thought on, vindictively, of those who were responsible for it always having been the same.

They, as far as Tom Brady was concerned, were what he had in England classified with uncertainty as intellectuals, meaning anyone higher on the ladder than himself—a foreman, a manager, a police sergeant, an army corporal. His uncertainty was removed in Australia, where unbeknownst to himself he had found safety in the fact of the Australians' traditional, unmalicious dislike of Englishmen, and so for twenty years had resisted thinking that he was, after all, ethnically a Gael; had, indeed, played up his Englishness to the extent of reviving and sticking doggedly to his Devonshire accent. Had he been a good enough mimic he would have talked like a B.B.C. announcer. Every little helped.

15

He turned his mind now on the latest outrage, being moved from one of the good front rooms in his boarding house to one of the back, on the flimsy excuse that his snoring disturbed his neighbours. Although Tom knew that he snored (his wife had slept with earplugs), he thought nothing of it because of the great and godlike compassion he had when it came to forgiving frailties of his own. The room's new tenant was, of course, Australian.

That everyone else in the house was also a native of the country Tom chose to ignore. And it was his usurper he was thinking of nastily as he approached the fish shop on George Street.

The coincidence of Jack Partridge also walking on George Street that same spring afternoon was not particularly odd, for of Sydney's main thoroughfare it might be said, as was said of Piccadilly Circus, Times Square and the Spanish Steps in Rome, that if you stood there long enough you would be sure to meet everyone you had ever known. Rather, the oddness lay in the fact that Tom Brady and Jack Partridge had lived within five miles of one another for so many years without having met before. Met, that is, for the second time; their first meeting, which lasted seven and a half seconds, took place in London some thirty years previously.

Jack Partridge was a fine-looking man for his age, fifty-eight, almost a good-looking man with his grey hair of military neatness, straight nose, firm mouth and chin, tall brow, attractive blue eyes, light suntan. What prevented his elevation to good looks was that very firmness of the lower face along with a general severity in manner, the carriage of his head, the set of his shoulders and the unflinching honesty of his gaze. People saw the disquieting rigidity instead of the features; they felt scruffy or vaguely criminal; they were glad to leave his presence.

Among those who knew him well there were no fence sitters, no one indifferent to his personality. By his acquaintances he was either liked or disliked, with the balance favouring the antis. Some said he was a fine man whose air of authority was reassuring. Others said he had no feelings, that if you cut him open you would find an adding machine inside. But he's honest, said some. So is a machine, said others. Some said he had a fine brain and was a thinker. Others said you couldn't go by appearances, a cow might look awfully contemplative while chewing the cud but its mind was really full of bull. Some said others were jealous. Others said some were intimidated. And nobody won. The chief argument remained Jack himself, who, well aware of the likers and dislikers, never gave a thought to influencing either one either way.

As he strode along through the shoppers he made a striking if unsympathetic figure. Tall, heavy yet paunchless, wearing a dark blue business suit and a light blue Panama, he looked to be at the very least a schoolmaster, and somehow the path ahead of him was always clear.

Typically, he ignored the window displays which presented themselves in a continuous stream at his side. He had come downtown for one reason only and that reason was not the admiration of window displays.

At length he turned into a shop, a gentlemen's outfitters, all old oak and thick carpets and hushed voices. Finding the counter he wanted, Jack Partridge asked of the suitably subdued salesman:

"Have you a white poplin shirt, button-down collar, neck size sixteen?"

"Yes, sir, we have, sir." With a bowing sweep the sales-

17

man turned to a stack of drawers, pulled one out and set it on the counter. "White poplin, button-down, sixteen."

Jack reached out a strong forefinger to poke the buttons, lift the front and scratch the cloth. "Seems a good shirt."

"An excellent shirt, sir."

"And the price, please?"

The salesman winced, as if people were not supposed to ask questions like that but simply say, "I'll take half a dozen." A trifle less subdued he told his customer that this was the top quality line selling at twelve dollars.

"There are other qualities?"

"Nine dollars and seven dollars."

"I'll take two of the nine, please."

Appeased, possibly at not having to handle the seven, said the clerk as he brought a pair of shirts from another drawer, "They also come in pale green. Extremely popular at the moment."

"Just the two white, please."

"Very good, sir. Handkerchiefs?"

Jack shook his head. "No, thank you."

"Socks?"

"No."

"We have a new shipment of knitted ties from Scotland?"

"If," said Jack Partridge, "I wanted a knitted tie from Scotland, I should ask for one."

"Yes," mumbled the salesman, his lip atwitch with loathing. "Sir."

Jack had spoken quite pleasantly. He was merely stating a fact. He most certainly would have asked for one had he wanted a knitted tie from Scotland. He thought it funny how some people could kid themselves that they knew what other people wanted. Imagine him saying to one of his customers, "Now don't tell me, I know you're dying to trade

18

your Holden in on that Dodge." Or, "Yes, sir, you want a valve job and a new crown wheel, I can see by your eyes." Or, "Six gallons of super and a quart of oil for you."

The salesman said, "That will be eighteen dollars, please."

Transaction completed, Jack Partridge took the paper bag under his arm, said a cheery good afternoon, received a muttered reply and strode from the shop.

He thought the salesman had looked put out, ruffled, irked. In searching for a reason, it occurred to him that it might have been on account of the ties. The man must have Scots blood, or even be actually Scottish. That was something you had to be careful of in a new country. A man could look like anyone else yet be, say, half Greek, half Swedish, and if you started talking, quite objectively of course, about Cypress or neutrality, you were liable to find yourself in trouble. Why couldn't everyone be objective? The salesman obviously was not.

Jack's step faltered. For a moment, a moment which many people would have enjoyed witnessing, he lost his look of purpose as he wondered should he return to the shop and say that he had nothing whatever against the Scots, that he probably had a drop or two of Scottish blood himself. He didn't want the salesman's feelings to be hurt.

Or, mused Jack, frowning, could there be another reason for the cold attitude? A worse reason? The reverse of what he was thinking? That the salesman thought *him* the foreigner. Or, being a Scot, hated him for a Sassenach.

Jack shook his head. There had been times in the past thirty years when this might have been a factor worthy of consideration, worthy of fear, times when he did doubt the efficacy of his act. Not any more. He was so completely Australian in every way that his former life, on the rare occasions that he gave it a thought, seemed to belong to

19

another man, as indeed it did, to Jack Armstrong (curious how alien the name sounded), the man who had been successfully put to death on the purchase of a passport from a drunk named Partridge.

No, the salesman's attitude came from the first assumption, and no, going back would be silly, embarrassing, making a slag heap out of a compost pile. Besides, the man had probably forgotten all about him by now.

Jack's step firmed, he gave a downward tug to the brim of his hat, he hitched up the paper bag. Once again he was Authority personified.

He smiled with satisfaction at having accomplished his mission, inconsequential though it was, with such ease and speed. Three minutes would see him back to the car, ten minutes back to work. Say half an hour in all. That would put his wife in her place.

When, last night, he had mentioned to Mildred that he needed a couple of shirts she had said:

"All right, dear. What kind shall I get for you?"

Fighting words, in the nicest possible way. Not that she meant she would use her own money, that point had been settled long ago; she meant she herself would do the buying, he selecting. This had never happened before. He shopped for his own clothes, as any real man should.

"Mil," he had said, "you're losing your sense of values."

"What does that mean?"

"You know. And it's because of that stupid television set. You've been watching too many of those Yank shows where the woman's the man of the house."

"Nonsense," she laughed. "I just wanted to save you hours of searching."

"Nonsense yourself. I'll do it just like that"—with a finger-snap. "Now how about another cold beer, please."

That had been the end of it. Jack realized, however, that lately Mildred had been exerting herself more and more in lots of little ways. Really, there were times when he was sure his wife thought herself almost an equal. Silly, but there it was.

Considering this, Jack began to feel uncomfortably that he was not being fair to his wife or the whole sex, that he had become a mite *too* Australian. Still feeling the same a minute later he veered to the inside of the pavement and bought a religious magazine from a girl with large, door-stopping feet and feverish eyes. He gave her his promise, retreating from the attack which followed the sale shock that yes, quite, certainly, he would read every word.

Another minute later, and a street photographer indiscriminately snapping all comers received, in exchange for one of the tickets he handed out, a magazine, which he tossed away in disgust because, for Christ's sake, it was about religion.

Jack Partridge, after also tossing away his part of the exchange, went back to thinking about his wife.

Although he had not been in love with Mildred when they married, he had come to love her in time. When they met, soon after his arrival from England and acquisition of a job in one of the bicycle stores owned by Mildred's father, there had been another girl he liked equally. Since he wanted to get married, and since he thought he might be too self-concerned to ever fall in love, he made his choice. He chose Mildred because she was the boss's daughter. He wanted to prove something to himself and disappoint people by not allowing them the pleasure of sneering, for he had no intentions of accepting money or help from his father-in-law.

With hardly even a shoestring for support he opened a

motorcycle repair shop in a rotting, leaky shed. By working sixteen hard hours a day he prospered. After two years he moved to better premises and took on an assistant. Continuing to prosper he opened another shop, then another, finally had six. Exempted from military service because of faulty vision, he won a government contract for vehicle servicing, and continued to prosper. In time he sold the chain and bought a garage, sold it for profit and bought another. Content now with his niche, he had no plans for further expansion. He was financially stable, with the added background security of a moneyed wife—she had long since come into her inheritance and Jack had long since laid down that her money was for their children; any buying or supporting to be done, he would do.

Jack Partridge was a solid citizen. He went to the local Baptist church every other Sunday, not because he believed in God but because he believed in setting a good example. He owned a home in sturdily middle-class Dimple Hill. He had aided Australia's population implosion by siring three sons who in turn had produced children of their own. He gave to worthy causes. He drank moderately. He ran his business with a hand firm yet kind, shrewd yet honest. He had never been unfaithful to his wife even in thought. He paid his taxes to the cent, was careful with water during shortages and in all respects obeyed the laws of the country. A solid citizen.

His only worry, that the dead past would come to life, had diminished with the years. He thought of it now only when reminded: a crime film, a newspaper report, and the occasional blood-spattered nightmare.

He swung along with the stride of a free man in his passage toward the fish shop.

If there was no coincidence in Tom Brady and Jack Partridge being on George Street that afternoon, there was perhaps something of a fluke in the presence there also of Mrs Janet Tree, insofar as she caused, in a way, the two men's second meeting.

Janet Tree lived in Dimple Hill, where she had a large house, far too large a house for her own small self, which situation she rectified by giving bed and breakfast to two gentleman boarders; never more than two, for otherwise she would have had to hire a maid, the payment of whose wages would have meant taking more boarders . . . and the thing would snowball into what Janet didn't want—a business. Her paying guests were there to fill space and comfort her with the knowledge that she was not alone in the house, not provide income. There was an easier way to get what she wanted, to buy what she needed.

Mrs Tree turned into a covered arcade of shops, a window-sided tunnel full of the clattering and echoing of the feet on its tile floor. A number of shops were fronted by tables that held special bargains, which is to say, soiled articles that refused to move unless glamourized by the bargain mystique.

By one of these tables Janet Tree stopped. A little hors d'oeuvre? she mused.

At the front were evening purses priced at three dollars, the foremost a packing-bloated skin of white sequins, like a pig in tight drag. Janet looked through the store window. There were two salesgirls, neither watching; one was busy applying make-up, the other stared at herself insolently in a mirror.

Janet stepped closer and put her gap-mouthed shopping bag under the table edge. She glanced to either side, slowly, not as if looking but as if roaming her head in cogitation as she considered making a purchase.

There were no lingerers and the crowd, streaming past at a steady pace, was close enough to Janet to not see her with clarity.

She put out a hand and tapped the white purse into her bag.

With another look through the window to check on safety (at this stage she could always say she intended paying; she was still here, wasn't she? she hadn't run away, had she?), Janet turned and walked on.

Her heart thudded uncomfortably and her back prickled, until she regained the street, when, growing calm, she wished she had taken two purses or even three.

She headed for her next regular call, face up to feel the gentle caress of the sun.

It was a small face, simian, large brown wondering eyes and blob nose and stretched mouth in pudgy flesh that had too many lines for its age, forty-two. She wore only a trace of lipstick, no jewellery and was careless about her mongrel-brown hair, which was youthfully short and wavy. Her large white teeth she showed often in a smile attractive but nervous, as if she were not sure she should be smiling at all. Unsmiling, she was not attractive, frumpy rather, with her short thin body dressed in dull clothes, a body inclined to be shrinking, as though it were saying touch-me-not.

Janet Tree was, altogether, a nervous sort of person, although not half so nervous as before her accidental discovery of what could be achieved through her hobby of acquiring—and where she got the courage to pursue this hobby was something she had never understood. Noises

24

made her jump, shrill voices made her cringe, fast traffic made her sheer away. She liked small animals and dumb children, books by polite lady novelists, playing soft-tuned chamber music on her radio, visiting friends in an old folks' home and knitting bedsocks that somehow always wanted to be scarves.

She considered the human body an embarrassment, its natural functions degrading. She had never looked in a mirror while naked, she thought of something else while blowing her nose and when in the lavatory closed her eyes and pretended herself a thousand miles away.

Janet's family had been cold in personal relationships and rich in personal comforts: prudes wearing cloth of gold, the Puritan ethos with Roman trappings. They were people whose thinking was a mixture of the dense and the bright, like that of someone who discovers that emordnilap spelt backwards is palindrome. They had turned their backs For Ever on Janet when she ran off from Perth to marry a soldier she had met in her capacity of Red Cross volunteer.

Having been brought up to be a lady, not a wage-earner, Janet was lucky in that her half-Italian husband had not been without means. Following a three week honeymoon of frightening passion, he went off to die in New Guinea. Janet became the owner of a house in Dimple Hill and a corporal's widow's pension.

Nowadays she had to look at a smudged photograph to recall what her husband looked like; after all, she had known him little more than a month. In fact she did not care too often to recall, finding his memory somehow shameful. When people in the early days commiserated with her over his death she had to nudge herself out of a blush and into a look of sadness. For twenty years she had been locked within the walls of her personal nunnery.

25

Janet Tree had no complaints, was satisfied with her lot, although she did possess two secret fears.

The first was that someday, somewhere, she would lose her drawers. Countless times had she pictured the scene. While the background changed—a street, a shop, the foyer of a theatre—there were always a great many people present, people with quick eyes, and she would be pausing in a space which they surrounded. One minute everything would be all right, the next—flop—there were her panties around her ankles. The laughter would roar and boom and whinny, and she would die, she would simply die.

Sometimes Janet would sit lost in her cruel daydream, unable to escape, squirming and sweating as she saw herself struggle to get free of the confining garment and listened horrified to the laughter. No one ever came forward to help.

Every morning when putting on her daily-fresh panties she secured them fore and aft with large safety pins. If startled, it was not her heart she grabbed for but her waist.

Her second fear, of course, was that she would be caught.

Janet Tree turned now in at the door of a department store. It was crowded, she was pleased to note. Last week (she visited no store more frequently than once a week), the place had been virtually empty, rendering operations dangerous, and she had been lucky to get a small sewing kit, a mere two-dollar value.

After a brief hesitation on the threshold, Janet made toward the left, choosing that way because during her pause she had spotted on the right a floorwalker, store detective. These she never had any trouble identifying. Physical attributes apart, they always acted so casually, the same supercasualness against which she was constantly warning herself, that they could only be detectives or thieves.

She browsed around several counters and handled goods she would not dream of acquiring, being too large or too cheap, in every case making a small fuss about returning the object to its place. The gambit was necessary here. This was no arcade with outside tables, child's play. This was a store with a hundred professional eyes.

Finally she chose to stop at a counter of clocks and watches. The sole salesgirl was occupied with customers. Janet moved to a section of twenty-dollar mantle clocks and brought her bag into position.

An interesting contraption, Janet's bag. Made of grey wool that could stretch amazingly, supported by rope handles, its mouth was held stiffly open in an oval shape by a stitched-in ring of wire. At one corner of the mouth, lying horizontal as if resting on something else beneath, was a ball of wool complete with two needles. A touch of genius here, for what could be more homely and old-fashioned, more an allayer of suspicion, than a bag of knitting?

Janet picked up a clock, admired its face, listened to its tick. A glance around, one which gave the impression of looking for sales attention, told her that the moment was right. She lowered the clock without haste to her bag. The wool and needles swung down to admit the clock: then swung up again.

Janet walked on, eyes blank as she strained her senses to catch, though fearing to catch, a hint of sound or movement or observation from behind. Nothing happened.

She spent close on an hour in the store, buying for cash, total outlay sixty-seven cents, a comb, a packet of balloons, a tube of toothpicks and a pencil, while acquiring for nothing a silver-plated tankard, a popular novel, a bottle of perfume, two flashlights and a necklace of cultured pearls.

27

Out in the street, she decided she had done well enough for one day. She would go shopping again tomorrow.

With interest she lingered by a fish shop, the retail department of the sea-food restaurant above. The shop sold delicacies such as octopus, squid, Isle of Man kippers. After watching the slow movements of a lobster, feeling for it a pang of pity, she moved on.

At which point she noticed a man standing on the kerb. He was looking at her fixedly.

For five seconds, five awful seconds, Janet Tree thought that this was It. She halted. Both hands clutched at her waistband. Apart from the man being familiar, he was a pastiche of every floorwalker she had ever carefully kept her distance from: big, older, with that stern ex-policeman look.

At the sixth second her rising panic snapped off. She realized the why of the familiarity. The man was a neighbour from Gormon Lane, Dimple Hill. What was his name now, Pheasant, Partridge? One of the two.

She stepped forward, answered his hesitant smile and said, "Good afternoon."

As he removed his hat, Jack Partridge was hurriedly thinking, Bush, Oaks, Greenwood . . .

"Mrs Tree," he said. "Good afternoon."

"Nice day."

"Indeed it is."

"Your wife is well, I trust?"

"Yes, Mrs Partridge is quite well, thank you. And"—not sure of the woman's connexions—"how's everything at your end of the street?"

"Fine."

"Well, that's fine, fine."

"Lovely day."

"Indeed it is."

"Now I must be off," said Mrs Tree. "Good afternoon."

"Good afternoon."

Jack looked back at the roadway. He had been about to cross when he had seen his neighbour. Now the opportunity was gone, traffic having closed in again.

So it was that he turned to walk on, hat still in hand, and came face to face with Tom Brady.

Recognition was instant. Each had been haunted by the face of the other for years.

They stopped.

They stared.

Both had the same feeling of shock, of outraged normalcy. But whereas Tom Brady's emotion continued at the same level, Jack Partridge's changed swiftly to fear.

And the meeting was over.

With an actual charge of pain in his chest Jack blundered on past, his stride ragged. Suddenly obeying the urge to run, hide, he dashed forward, scattering people, his hat gripped in one outpushed hand, his paper bag in the other. He turned into a shop, crashed into and knocked over a salesgirl and ran to the rear amid gasps of alarm.

Jack Partridge was no longer recognizable as the man of purpose he had been one minute before. His body flapped loosely, his teeth showed in the ridiculous grin of fright, his eyes were round and stupid.

He burst through a doorway into a yard, across it and

through a gate and into an alley, where he broke into a frantic run.

Tom Brady still stood in the same place, still shocked immobile. He could hardly believe it was true. Again he had seen the face of murder.

2

Some five hundred yards long, lying like the bar in an H between two similar residential streets, Gormon Lane might have been in a suburb of Manchester or Bournemouth were it not for the eucalyptus trees spaced along the kerbs, the odd roof of corrugated tin, one date palm and the water sprinklers on every lawn. Without exception the houses and bungalows were of red brick. Many windows took the form of bays, some were even leaded. Names were preferred to numbers: "Happy Days," "Bide-a-Long," "Trailends." It was a disappointment not to find a "Dunroamin." Gormon Lane was that kind of street.

"The Pear Tree" had in the centre of its lawn a frail sapling supported contemptuously by a stout stave, as a constable might support a weaving, weakling drunk. Like Peter Pan, the tree had never grown up or borne fruit. It had been planted solely that the house could with honesty be given its name, which would match with the old carol whose oft repeated line put a partridge firmly and permanently in its place.

A bungalow, "The Pear Tree" had been face-lifted to look five years old instead of the true forty. False shutters had been fixed beside those windows visible from the road and the main window had been enlarged to picture size, the door had become a flat surface of white and the driveway that ran beside the house was now laid with crazy paving.

Gormon Lane showed its fortunate lack of consequence as a traffic artery in the swells, cracks and jagged breaks which the tarmac had been allowed to develope; and not until these irregularities were shaking the suspension of his car did Jack Partridge realize where he was, realize that without thinking he had driven straight home instead of to work.

It was too late to drive away again. In any case, home was where he wanted to be. He slowed, steered smoothly with the precision of settling panic around a child's tricycle lying in the road and turned into his driveway.

Stopping by the garage doors he automatically switched off the engine and pulled on the hand brake. He made no move to get out. He sat, staring ahead. His body was tense, trembling, his palms and brow wet. Instinct made him shrink down in the seat. He thought it incredible that he had got safely away from George Street, forcing himself from a run to a walk so as not to attract attention. Incredible, he thought, which kept him from thinking the worst.

"Jack?"

He looked around slowly. Through the kitchen window his wife was watching. Although he tried first a smile and then a word, he managed neither.

Mildred went from the window, came outside. She was a tall woman with straight greying hair drawn back loosely into a pony-tail. Her pleasant face was now rendered plain by a twist of anxiety. Striding to the car she pulled open the door.

"Jack? What's wrong?"

He couldn't even begin to explain. All he wanted to do, still, was hide. He forced out, "Feel a bit crook."

"You're trembling," she said, offended.

"A chill."

"Sweating too. Feverish as anything."

"A chill. I'll get to bed."

"I should just think you would. And quick's the word. I'll phone the doctor."

"No, Mil." He got heavily out of the car. "No you won't. Aspirins."

"Oh, you," said Mildred. "You will have your own way." She was successfully turning her anxiety into annoyance at Jack's childishness and at the impertinence of his fever.

Jack allowed himself to be towed by the hand inside and through to a bedroom, where Mildred tutted and fussed while he undressed. She brought aspirins, frowned them on their way down, ushered him into bed, drew the curtains and went out with a final grumble of exasperation.

Immediately, Jack felt a fast-climbing nausea. Leaping from bed he went in silent speed to the bathroom and fell to his knees by the lavatory. He let the vomit gush. His stomach tore with pain as it fought to reject its thirty years of poison.

Drained, he weakly wiped his mouth, rose and made a quiet return.

With the covers pulled over his head he nestled down, curling himself into a foetal ball, knees up, arms crossed on his chest, hands cuddled under his chin. It was a position he had not assumed since forgotten childhood and which normally he would have considered odious, spineless, fey. Now he gave it no thought. He felt safer.

At length his trembling stopped. The shock of fear passing, he became filled with the same emotion's deadness. He accepted without quarter or question that his life was essentially over. Children, grandchildren, wife, business, home, freedom—these were of the past. There was nothing left. All he could say was that he had stolen thirty years. It was simply a matter of short time before the end was signalled by a hard knock on the door.

They might come in an hour, they might be walking up the drive this minute.

When another bout of trembling had passed, Jack forced himself for the sake of peace to examine the situation in less dramatic, more mundane terms. First, was there any question about the man on George Street? No. Nor was there any question of recognition the other way. Could it then not merely be a fantastic coincidence that they should meet but the hoped-for end of X's search? That itself was fantastic. The authorities would have long since closed the case, so why should one disinterested man, not brother, cousin, lover, why should he spend a lifetime in pressing the investigation?

Apart from the unfeasibility of this, there was nothing for the man to investigate.

No relative or friend had come forward to claim the body.

The renting agent knew nothing about the husband.

He was unknown to the neighbours.

There was nothing to connect him with the scene except his face and a false name, the first one.

Really, Jack thought, it could have been no better had he planned the whole thing. He had been amazingly lucky. And his luck had held when he turned to the solution: remove their only clue, his face. Which meant leaving the country, which meant false papers, there being a fear at the time that his true name might somehow be unearthed.

Since he lacked the connexions, and the time to make same, through which he might have been able to get papers forged, Jack had set out to buy or steal another's identity,

34

preferably Canadian, having always fancied a try at the Prairies. As an interim disguise, after moving into a low lodging house, he let his beard grow to a stubble and affected the dress of a navvy—slouch hat, corduroys tied at the knees with string, muddied boots—and in daylight went around with a spade on his shoulder. No one ever gave him a second glance. Even when a sketch of his face (an excellent likeness) appeared in the newspapers as being the man whom the police believed could help with their investigation, no one looked at him twice. And if the sketch was ever supplied with a name it was never given to the public.

By making circumspect enquiries in what he considered the right places, of those he considered the right people, with the story that he had been working against the bloody English for the Irish Republican Army, he came at length to an Australian two years older than himself who was drinking his life away in the pubs of Earl's Court. A passport eagerly changed hands for the equivalent of a week's drink. That the photograph bore not the slightest resemblance Jack thought unimportant. That the Australian's first name was John struck a lucky note, for Jack could go on calling himself Jack, which left much less margin for error, for forgetfully answering to the wrong name.

After selling his wristwatch and solitaire ring he booked passage for Sydney. Though by this time there was no longer any mention of the case in the newspapers, he took no chances. In a spruced-up version of his navvy role, looking in fact, with a steerage ticket and paper parcel luggage, the perfect Colonial who had failed to strike it rich in the land of his fathers, he presented himself at Tilbury one cold morning for embarkation. His passport was skimmed through and he got aboard the liner. During the six-week voyage he kept to himself but eavesdropped on every conversation about the country to which he was headed, gathering information. At Sydney he landed without trouble. He was free.

John Partridge had been from Wagga Wagga, too close to Sydney for comfort. Jack told anyone who asked that he was from Darwin. The identity was never questioned, and until he perfected his accent, which came easily, blending with his non-H-dropping polite cockney, he laughed off mistakes as being the result of too long a stay in Britain.

By subscribing to a London daily for three years he found final security in a four-line item to the effect that one John Henry Partridge, an Australian, had been discovered dead of natural causes in a railway shack and buried by Australia House.

No, Jack thought, there could have been no following up of clues. The meeting on Geroge Street had been a hideous fluke. Not that it mattered. The damage was done. He had been recognized. The man would have gone to the police. This time their task would be simplified. How many men of his description could have been known to be shopping today on George Street? And the description could not be made useless. Disguise was out. He could not run now. It was just a matter of time.

At the opposite end of Gormon Lane to the Partridge bungalow and on the opposite side stood "West Wind," a sombre house of dark green paintwork. There were two piles of bay windows, like three-tier cakes without icing, separated by a porticoed door and a balconied french window and a sundial that had stopped, its point having rotted off. The pretentiousness of the place was apparent only from an end view, when its lack of depth was seen: a big-chested soldier with a hollow back.

Nevertheless, Mrs Janet Tree, reaching the end of the five yards of path, glanced back with a look of pride and approval at her house. It was all she had in the world and she loved it as an actor loves his profile.

She passed through the gateway or ornamental iron, frowning at its squeak, and headed for the bus stop.

Once home from her outing downtown, Janet had decided that as the day was young she might as well see her broker. She had changed into a plum-coloured coat, transferred her items to an ordinary carrier bag and added the pair of binoculars from a previous outing.

On a main road she caught a bus. Ten minutes later she alighted and caught another, rode for five minutes, got off, walked six blocks, waited a while and got on her third and last bus. The journey could have been realized with less outlay of time, money and effort if she had gone by underground train; but the subway Janet found unnerving with its rush and crush and vastness. She felt too anonymous, which, except when on acquiring trips, was not to her liking.

Also not to her liking was the place where she at last left her bus. It was a commercial district close to the docks, noisome and tough. On the seedy sides were pubs, seamen's missions, tenements, pawnbrokers and chandlers; at ground level were dusty cars and broken flotsam, piles of crates and ice cream carts; above were leaning poles playing cats-cradle with a million wires of worrisome complexity. The human element was lounging men, foreign sailors, and groups of children who looked in need of a rich, young, healthy country in which to grow up.

Janet, almost without being conscious of the act, crossed the road to avoid one such group of children, crossed back again and dabbed her handkerchief to her nose to counter the smell of fish and tar and cinder fumes. After cringing her way past a cafe whose open door was blasting out a garble of music, she came to a halt.

She was standing before a shop which displayed above its window the sign of a fugitive from the temple: the three golden promises forever suspended beyond reach: the innocents' symbol of faith in their hope of charity.

Seeing through the window that Mr Beeker the pawnbroker was busy with a client, Janet walked slowly on.

No innocent she, Janet Tree's hopes were pinned on getting thirty per cent of retail value, a value which Mr Beeker by some miracle could always guess to within half a dollar.

Mr Beeker was what Janet knew to be called a fence, a receiver of stolen goods; she also knew that he sold mostly to sailors, who took the goods away into the cold. He was, of course, a criminal. Janet felt that while it was unfortunate to have to associate with such a type, it was much safer than going repeatedly to different shops, where too many questions might be asked and suspicion aroused. There was security in Mr Beeker knowing the truth.

Some years before, following Janet's first adventure in free shopping, she had come to this district because she had heard it contained any number of pawnbrokers and had chosen Beeker & Son at random. She offered for sale an assortment of "unwanted birthday presents." Mr Beeker bought. Two days later he bought again. On the third visit he said with a charming smile that henceforth he would pay one quarter of the original value and would she tell her friends to send gifts of watches and cameras, there was always a good market for watches and cameras, to send nothing in the clothing line and no more sets of teaspoons please.

They understood one another. Their dealings were more

on the level of a social event, a neighbourly call. Their sole point of disagreement lay between twenty-five per cent and thirty.

To that first adventure Janet's mind now went back. It had started with a mistake. She had gone to the department store specifically to buy one of the table lighters they were advertizing as that week's special. At the counter she spent some time in choosing the design she wanted, and only when she had left, was halfway down the store with the lighter in her bag, did she realize she had forgotten to pay. She went back. The salesgirl was busy, refused to have her eye caught or to hear coughs and calls. Janet took another lighter, for spite. She returned later to take another for profit.

Turning, she strolled back to the shop. It was empty. As she entered, Mr Beeker appeared in a curtained doorway beyond the counter. He was short, stout and Pickwickian, with a round red face of sixty or so topped by feathery white hair; a face whose pleasantness Janet, knowing its occupation, sometimes found vaguely offensive.

"Good afternoon, Mrs Jones," he said, smiling, innuendoing as usual the name.

"Good afternoon, Mr Beeker."

"How's everything out Wollongong way?"

"Very well, thank you. And the rheumatism?"

"Lying low, touch wood."

"That's a blessing."

"Well, if you'll fix the door, Mrs Jones, and come in. I've got the kettle on."

After snicking home a bolt and turning over a card that said *Back in 15 Mins,* Janet went through into the Edwardian parlour—scrolled mahogany, plush cloths with bobbles, specimens of taxidermy, electrified oil-lamps, and unnecessary fire in a cast-iron grate.

She sat at a table, bowed into place by Mr Beeker, who then also sat. He rubbed his hands together (which hint of commerce Janet disapproved of) before lighting up a long black panatella (which gained Janet's approval because it went so well with his frontiersman look of striped shirt with garters and flowered weskit). He said:

"Well now, mm?"

Commenting in a mild, ladylike, restrained way on the good points and high value of each acquisition as she drew it out, Janet leisurely emptied her bag.

Mr Beeker smiled at the tankard and binoculars, nodded cheerfully at the flashlights, necklace and clock, shrugged with indifference at the perfume, shook his head in bewilderment at the novel, and switched from the evening purse to Janet a look of reproach.

"It's a pretty little purse," she said, not as sales talk but in self-consolation, knowing by the other's attitude that at Chrismastime she would be given the purse back as a present.

Mr Beeker shook his head again at the novel. He murmured, "Those friends of yours . . ."

"They are apt to forget once in a while," Janet agreed.

"Well, I suppose I can always give it to the Salvation Army."

"You're such a generous man, Mr Beeker."

The pawnbroker hurriedly cleared his throat. The forefinger and thumb pincers of either hand assaulted his weskit pockets until they came up with a stubby pencil and a scrap of paper. He began to scribble. The result he slid across for inspection.

Janet did some mental arithmetic. She found that the

sum on the paper was thirty-six cents short of being a neat one quarter of the total value of the goods. Nonplussed by the man's brilliance, she merely sighed, "Very well."

After counting out dollars, Mr Beeker busied himself with making tea.

Janet put the money away. She forgot business. She experienced a tickling trill of pleasure up her spine as she thought of the orgy ahead.

Tom Brady was far from George Street and far from home.

When jolted by the passing crowd out of his immobility he had set off walking, heading in any direction which presented itself. Pace slower than normal and the fingers of his rear-clasped hands lying placid, stunned, he had slooped along without the slightest awareness of his surroundings.

Now, at last, his stupefaction was fading. He had long since stopped raising his eyebrows and shaking his head, stopped questioning the evidence of his eyes, stopped mumbling, "Impossible." Now he even stopped being surprised.

Yes, he had seen the murderer. Thirty years older but definitely the same man. Hardly changed at all in fact, except for the grey hair. There was no mistake, you could see the man was shocked himself, recognizing and knowing he had been recognized.

Tom gave one last shake of his head, during which he came aware of being in strange territory. At a faster walk he looked around, looking for landmarks. Soon he got his bearings, made a drastic change in course and set off for home.

Thirty years, he mused. A lifetime. Even so, the memory was as clear as clear.

Tom not only remembered the day, a Tuesday, August

twenty-seventh, he remembered the weather—mild, with a hint of rain. Even at eleven that night it had still been warm.

Police Constable Thomas Brady felt in good spirits as he left the Station to stride out his rounds on the graveyard shift. In fine weather the nightbeat was a welcome change: you could have a quiet smoke, there was little to do and in this part of London the untoward was unusual, the violent a rarity. Another reason for his high humour was that he had recently completed his first year on the force and was sure he had made a good impression. With luck, he would soon begin his climb.

Back in from Cromwell Road the residential streets were quiet and all but deserted. Tom frowned sternly at two home-winding drunks, tested the door of an occasional shop, turned his gaze from panting couples in doorways, whistled under his breath, listened to the sound of his measured tread and took pride in the knowledge that all around him others were also listening and drawing comfort therefrom.

The thing began at about midnight (twelve minutes to, it was later established). He was passing a block of flats when from above came a woman's scream. Jerking to a stop he looked up.

Although short, the scream had been full of harsh horror. Indeed, its very shortness added to the horrific impression, suggesting as it did a malicious truncating rather than a natural wailing off.

When Tom looked up only one window in the block was with light. Almost at once another window showed where it stood. A minute passed. There was no more sound. Another minute and the second light went out. Still no more sound.

Tom moved to front the entrance of the flats, a recessed

doorway with head-height lamps on either side. He felt both relieved and disappointed, thinking, as obviously the owner of the second window had thought, that the scream must have been caused by something innocuous: a nightmare, a spider, perhaps a game.

Yet for some reason he stayed on, standing at the doorway. He was not surprised when, following another minute or two of silence, he heard from beyond the door a rapid thudding, like someone running down stairs.

He took one wavering step backwards.

The footfalls grew louder, the door crashed open, a man rushed out—and stopped, teetering back from his speed.

The lamps shone their stark illumination on both faces, which were separated by no more than five feet. Tom saw the man's features with clarity and marked them well, despite a tendency to look instead at the blood. There were red, fresh, wet splotches scattered over his face and on his collar.

Out of force of officially encouraged habit, Tom also took in the other's clothes, the blue pin-stripe suit cut expensively in the latest style—high, square shoulders, broad lapels, wasp waist, twenty-two inch trouser cuffs—the neat collar and tie, the diamond on one finger and the pointed suede shoes.

The man broke into a run.

Tom watched him go, watched his frantic figure flash in and out of view among the lamps spread down the long road and then fade altogether as the sound of his passage had faded.

Tom looked back at the entrance. It seemed quiet and lawful. But that blood, he thought. And the man's look of fear. Plus the fact that he had run away.

Even so, the explanation could be innocent, or at least,

43

no one's business but the man's. An argument with his wife, an object thrown, a cut on his head, a slamming out of the flat to put an end to it all. The sort of thing that happened all the time. Later there would be a return, tears, a happy reconciliation.

Except that cuts didn't splash, not on the person cut, they ran.

Tom looked up. Again there were two windows alight. Conscious of an ache of excitement at the pit of his stomach, he went inside the building, to the stairs and up to the second floor, treading quietly.

As he turned onto a hallway he saw ahead an open door and beyond it a woman standing at another door, this one closed. Hair in curling rags, wearing a robe over a night-dress, of late middle-age, the woman was tapping and hissing, "Hello? Hello? Are you all right?"

At a cough from Tom she swung round with a frightened gasp, sagging and closing her eyes in relief on seeing the uniform. Tom went forward.

"What's going on here?" he asked, his voice low, his tone less authoritative than inquisitive.

In a flustery whisper the woman told of hearing the sounds of a fierce argument ending in a scream. "I got up," she said. "But then there was nothing else so I went to bed again. The next thing I knew he was leaving in ever such a hurry so I got up again."

"The husband?"

"I suppose so. And I just saw someone running down the street. Anyway, there's no sound from in there now. There should be, you know. She should be crying or something. Queer, I'd say, constable."

"This has happened before?"

44

"Oh, all the time. You wouldn't believe. But not as bad as now. That scream and everything."

"D'you know these people, ma'am?"

"No. I've never even seen them. You don't with neighbours these days, do you?"

Tom knocked. He knocked three times, the last a heavy bashing with the side of his fist. When a door farther along opened he told the face that looked out, "Police business." The face went.

Tom felt important enough to make a major decision. He would break in. Or rather, force an entry. He told himself that the circumstances demanded he do this. The woman inside might be badly injured, perhaps bleeding to death.

The door looked fragile; and was. On the first charge of his shoulder the wood flew in with a cheap tinkle and crackle. Revealed was an entrance hall the size of a telephone kiosk.

"That's the living room in there," whispered the woman, pointing to the light showing down the side of a door which stood an inch ajar. "It's right next to my bedroom and I can—"

Tom cut her off with a curt, "Stay here." One stride took him to the door. He eased it open. Lying inside, on her back, was the woman of the scream.

She was dead, this he knew even before he stooped to feel for a pulse. Her body and hair and clothes gave the impression of youth. Her face gave no impression whatever. It was a lumpy red mess.

Holding down his nausea and excitement, Tom stepped carefully over a glistening poker and returned to the neighbour. He told her what had happened and asked her to telephone the police station. Inside again, he lit a cigarette with unsteady hands, turned his back on the body and

45

thereby on his nausea, and allowed his excitement to grow.

He was in. He was in!

Tom Brady of the present sighed. He sighed heavily, while his fingers, which until a second ago had been rattling a nervous tattoo, began a fretful stroking motion.

That, he mused, had been the most important happening of his life. And what had come of it? Nothing, that's what. Bloody nothing.

He saw that he had again taken the wrong direction. With the vigour of annoyance he scratched at his tight white curls while swaying his large self around. He crossed a street, walked along to a corner, paused at a bus stop, decided he was not in the mood for standing still and kept on walking.

Bringing out his cigarettes he counted to see how many he had left. More than he expected, but, refusing to be pacified, he lit up grumpily. He went back to musing on his moment of fame that never came.

The day after the murder he found himself a person of consequence in Division B. He alone could give an accurate description of the husband, Peter Capstan. The agent who had leased them the flat seven weeks before and the two tenants who recalled seeing them in passing, had only the murkiest idea of what either of the Capstans looked like.

Taken off regular duties, Tom was assigned to the detectives working on the case. He went with them everywhere, he attended dozens of identification parades, twice he visited Scotland Yard to look at what seemed a million photographs and he told his story to attentive audiences at least fifty times. He was certainly the centre of attention.

Not that it was sugar all the way. He got reprimanded for not having telephoned the Station himself, with a pick-up order on the husband, as soon as he had found the body; precious time had been wasted when Capstan had no doubt been still in the area. And why hadn't he questioned the man in the first place? Also, how dare he smoke a cigarette at the scene? There were other odds and ends too such as touching things in the flat that were frowned upon; but in the main, things were golden.

The murder was the third biggest story of the moment, after an industrial strike and a French politician's divorce trial, and although Tom had not been mentioned in the newspapers, being forbidden by those higher up to talk to journalists, his big day would blossom later when they caught the husband.

Which, however, was slow in coming about. Mr and Mrs Capstan, assuming that as their real name, seemed to be completely without a past. They had never been heard of by anyone anywhere, their references for the flat proved to be forged, Somerset House had no record of their births or marriage, there was nothing on record to match with the fingerprints picked up in the flat.

The woman's face was beyond reconstruction and her teeth had received only the barest dental work, she had no surgical scars or physical peculiarities and had never borne children, her clothes were good but mass produced and she had no papers.

Nor had the man left papers behind, nor were his off-the-peg clothes any the less untraceable. His disappearance was absolute. When the Press published a likeness sketched from Constable Brady's description, the result was merely a downpour of false leads.

Weeks passed, the case was dropped from the newspapers; months passed, the case was eased into official limbo.

It was generally agreed that most likely the Capstans

were foreigners, probably a prostitute and her pimp who had come, as had thousands of others, legally and otherwise, to take advantage of London's favourable rate for flesh. The man would have returned to his own country.

Back on regular duties, Tom once in a while reminded his colleagues of the murder which he had unearthed. They hid their jealousy under a pretense of disinterest, even amusement. Worse lay ahead. When he came at last to broaching the topic of a promotion for himself he was amazed to learn that he was the only one who thought it deserved or desirable.

He never had his day. He never found his murderer. He was still a constable when he left to join the Army.

It had been a bitter experience. He had smelt the bouquet of the wine of greatness without being able to drink.

Tom's chin sank, his fingers stroked one another sympathetically.

The next moment he shot alert with a bright blink. He had almost forgotten the event of the day—the incident on George Street. Once more he was in the running for something big.

He grinned. He put his hands in and out of every pocket.

The better to savour his excitement and pleasure, he stopped for a minute. His grin grew and he shivered. Treating himself to a cigarette he went on, at which point he got a thought.

He wondered, for the first time, why he was walking toward home, why immediately after seeing Capstan he had not gone to the police.

While wondering, he continued walking toward home.

Presently he concluded that although he didn't know why, there must be a reason and he therefore had some serious thinking to do.

48

At dusk, Jack Partridge was lying straight out in bed, rigid, from his toes to his throat the covers drawn in tight seams, like a narrow field deeply ploughed. He ached in every part with waiting.

Why hadn't they come? his mind groaned. It was four or five hours now. Why the delay? Were they checking with London? Checking on the identity? Or were they hiding outside, perhaps wanting an escape attempt? If so, it was cruel, a form of torture. And unfair. The whole thing was unfair. After all, he was innocent of any crime.

3

Janet Tree awoke, as always, with a smile on her small, lined face. She sat up, luxuriated in a yawn and looked with satisfaction around her room, which, while to Janet comfortable, would to most people have been disconcerting in its neatness.

Each strip of the block-pattern wallpaper was matched with inhuman skill. The white tassels of the Bokhara carpet lay on their background of dark wood as symmetrical as rows of the shrouded dead. Wardrobe, chest of drawers, vanity table and bed of single width were matching and placed equidistant one from another. The nightstand held a clock, a lamp and four books of light verse, the two upright chairs which guarded the door stood an exact inch from the wall, not a wrong fold showed in the curtains and the six hunting prints were all of a size.

It was like a setting hurriedly put together to be looked at but not touched in a furniture exhibition. You felt that if you sat on a chair, lifted a book or misaligned one of the carpet's tassels, the whole ensemble would fall apart.

Yet Janet looked around with satisfaction. She did like things to be orderly. Order and routine, there was nothing finer, or safer, or more comforting. Though it was not always possible to keep the rest of the house in apple-pie shape,

here was inviolate, sanctuary, an oasis of trimness as un-
changingly true as the stars. She felt, she really did, that if
some morning she awoke to find her order gone she would
have a stroke. The same with routine, in lesser degree. If
she didn't know that she had this to do, followed by that,
and everything just so, she would be lost.

A glance at the bedside clock told Janet she had five
minutes to go. She always came awake before the eight
o'clock alarm went off, out of nervousness, afraid of being
startled by that sudden clamour; but equally afraid of being
late, which she had never been in her life, she dutifully set
the alarm every night.

For four and three-quarter minutes she thought about
the day ahead. After breakfast, a tidy round the house,
washing and ironing, and seeing to the rooms upstairs, she
would go out. That new department store was due for
another visit. She would try for a camera, really try hard
(poor Mr Beeker and those books and things). She would
go to the camera counter and take one just like snap. Except that it was never quite that easy. Operations downtown needed bravery, which she was sure she didn't have.
Still, when the time came to operate, she operated. Never
had she returned empty-handed. She supposed it was because this was something emotion made her do so that she
could indulge herself later. This craving . . . er . . .

Janet's thoughts stuttered off into incoherence as the
clock's minute hand crept closer to the perpendicular. She
fixed on the clock large wary eyes. She was not about to let
herself be caught off guard by the alarm. On the other hand
she was not going to drop the plunger to kill the alarm before birth for then she would have no way of knowing if
it would have gone off if she had not dropped the plunger.

And if it failed to go off, and if she had happened to have overslept . . . You had to be careful.

Features stiffening, body as tense as a paratrooper's as he waits for the signal to jump, Janet reached toward the clock as its hand made another uprighting twitch. With her nerves in a jangle she fought the urge to drop the plunger now, at once. She held on, hand at the dithering ready and eyes aglare.

One second before the final twitch, when the alarm was giving a faint preliminary clink, like the hissing intake of breath which precedes a bellow, Janet slapped the clock on its head. She relaxed with an unsteady laugh and got out from under the blankets.

The first thing she did, even before donning slippers and robe, was make her bed, performing the act until she had achieved some semblance of neatness, with her eyes slightly averted from the rumple. The final result would have brought praise from the crabbiest hospital matron.

On returning from her private bathroom Janet dressed in her usual dowdy clothes, not forgetting the two safety pins underneath, which reposed overnight in an otherwise empty pincushion hanging inside the wardrobe. Topping her dark dress with a dark apron, she went out of her room.

To Janet belonged the bottom third of the house. In addition to her bedroom with bath, she had a parlour with kitchen, these sections separated by a gloomy hall where a staircase led to the quarters of her two boarders; the top third of the house was empty.

In her kitchen she set about preparing breakfast: corn flakes, boiled eggs, toast, marmalade, tea. Mr East had a blue tray and Mr Snow had a green. That way there was never any confusion when everything was set out and ready for delivery; before, during preparation, Janet had every detail quite clear.

Mr East was three and a half minutes, Mr Snow four. Mr East was thick butter, Mr Snow medium. Mr East was one for the pot, Mr Snow none. Both wanted milk but Mr Snow was no sugar. Where almost any other landlady would have been exasperated by such details, Mrs Tree found them pleasant, part of the security of routine; the more detailed, the more value it had as something real. In any case, being fond of her boarders she liked to do them well. Mr Snow was a theological student of twenty-two cautious years, as grave as a bank. Mr East, a middle-aged assistant to a funeral director, was even graver. Two more respectable gentlemen would have been hard to find.

Trays ready, Janet put one on top of the other and carried them out of the kitchen and up the Turkey-red stair-carpet. The green tray she set down at Mr Snow's door, on which she tapped three times before moving along the hall.

As she was stooping with the blue tray Mr East swung his door open, and Janet knew by this that he had an early duty call. Straightening, handing him his breakfast, she asked, "Who is it?"

"Georgette Ricci," he said, "the comedienne. Good morning, Mrs Tree."

"Good morning. She was famous, wasn't she?"

"Quite. As you know, we rather tend to do the better people."

Mr East was small, not much taller than his landlady, nor with much more flesh. The severity of his morning suit—striped trousers, black jacket—was matched by a narrow parrot face whose tiny eyes of a glittering blackness seemed to squint as they sought to join in focus beyond the suprasenatorial nose. A redeeming feature was his richly dark, wavy hair with its angel-white wings.

"Yes," said Janet. As usual when talking to her paying guest she had to suppress a desire to suggest that if he turned his head sideways he would get a far better sighting. "It's quite at the top, your firm."

"*Service*," he reproved gently.

Janet was unabashed. "Yes, I'm pleased with you and Mr Snow. Both doing so well and everything."

"And," said Mr East, "I'm sure I can speak for Mr Snow when I say that we are pleased with our, shall I say, chatelaine."

"That's kind of you. But you're worth taking good care of. I've not always been so lucky with my residents as I have with Mr Snow and yourself."

"No?"

"Absolutely not. The gentleman before you, for instance, in this very room. Did you know that I had to ask him to leave?"

"No, I didn't."

"Well, I did. It was because of something I found here one morning when I came in to clean."

With an eagerness which showed itself only in a tightening of the thin mouth, Mr East leaned forward over his tray, looking like a waiter serving bedmates in a brothel. "Yes?"

"Disgusting."

"What did you find, Mrs Tree?"

"They were on the dressing table."

"What?"

"I can hardly bring myself to tell you, Mr East."

"*Try*, Mrs Tree."

"Well, all right," said Janet, and shuddering at the memory brought out the word in a suitably low voice:

"Toenails."

Mr East was aghast. They shook their heads at one another in silence.

When Tom Brady entered the dining room the other lodgers had eaten and gone. The one long table was a mess of slopped tea, full ashtrays, balled paper napkins and plates on which faint streaks indicated the recent presence there of food.

As Tom sat himself at the head of the table, not his normal place, a gaunt woman with muscular bare arms came in from the kitchen. Seeing Tom, she stopped and pointed an accusing finger. "You're late," she said.

Tom, after a slow, deliberate blink, said, "Yes, that's right, I am."

The woman stared, her arm drooping, like a man's nationalism when he is back from abroad.

Tom went on, "Nice and hot, my tea, please."

The woman turned and went out, frowning anxiously her surprise.

Tom was surprised himself. His usual attitude toward the stern proprietress of the boarding house was one of semi-humility, and in the event of being late for a meal, one of humility pure. But he had been feeling and acting quite differently this morning, ever since getting out of bed, when, instead of rushing down to get first grab of whatever was going, he had shaved with unaccustomed care, spent some minutes raising a shine on his boots, shook the dust off his jacket and even went so far as to ignore his muffler and put on a tie.

Odd, he thought. Perhaps it came from staying awake so long last night, discussing with himself the present situation. Not that he felt tired. He felt fit and bright. And nothing definite had been resolved, only that he should find Capstan and make sure of the identification before thinking about what the next step would be.

His breakfast came, steak and eggs and potatoes. He examined it critically, leaned back and gave the waiting woman a cool nod of approval. "Yes. Thank you."

She looked away, collected plates and hurried out.

Half an hour later, Tom left the house and set off to walk into town. He walked at a faster pace and in a more upright posture than normal. His arms swung at his sides. Once he squared his shoulders, and once, patting his paunch, he told himself he would have to try and get back into shape, there was no sense in going to pot when with a little effort he could be as fit as he had been during his prime years.

In the bustle of George Street Tom made straight for the fish shop. His cheerfulness was joined by a murmur of excitement. He stood with his back to the window and looked around. People, traffic. He waited.

He waited fifteen minutes before beginning to wonder why. What did he expect, another appearance by Capstan? Well, the idea was not too ridiculous. He might work around here somewhere, pass by any number of times a day.

Tom waited. He nodded at several faces he knew, pretended not to see the man who came out of the fish shop to stare at him pointedly for a full minute, smoked three cigarettes and shook his head apologetically at an aborigine of outback shabbiness who shuffled up to ask for the price of a sandwich.

The last event added to Tom's good cheer. No one had tried to put the bite on him in years. He made another attempt at squaring his shoulders.

A traffic skirmish set him to musing on the time he had witnessed an accident hereabouts. It had been something of an adventure and highly satisfying. He had been interviewed by the insurance people, bought drinks by the friendly side and given hard looks by the enemy. Later he had appeared in court, and although not one of the dozens of acquaintances he told about it showed up to watch . . .

Tom shook off the reminiscence. He told himself that this would never do. He was not keeping his mind on the job. Searching faces, he waited.

A clock struck eleven. Tom checked it with his pocket watch and decided he was getting nowhere. He moved on, mulling over his next move. Should he work at tracing Capstan backwards or forwards from the meeting? More important, how?

His hands had gone behind his back and his fingers were straying toward one another, as old minds stray to the comfort of the past, when he saw facing in the opposite direction a squat man on the kerb, aiming a camera at the approaching people.

Tom nodded to himself briskly. The street photographer, who was one of his pals-in-passing, might have the perfect answer to his problem: a snapshot. It could be carried around and shown to people in all parts of the city. Sooner or later someone would say, "Yes, I know him very well. Strange man that. You can tell there's some mystery in his past, a terrible crime maybe." Or something.

Tom stopped beside his friend. "Morning, morning."

"Morning," said the squat man, looking up from his aim. "Nice day for the race."

"Er, what race?"

"The *yuman* race!" the man managed to gasp before he choked on a wheezy laugh, which he helped out by pressing a fist into his side.

Tom smiled appreciatively.

The photographer became abruptly serious, like a school-boy scared from mirth by a teacher's stare, lifted and aimed and clicked his camera, pulled a ticket from a wad and handed it to a passer-by. Business over, he asked:

"Not a bad joke, eh?"

"Very funny. I can never remember them."

"It's a knack."

"Yes," said Tom. "Listen. Were you here yesterday afternoon?"

"Course. Every afternoon."

"Good. Well, listen. A mate of mine came by this way and I was wondering if you took his picture."

"Could have."

"I'd like to get it, see. Give it him as a present."

"Maybe he sent in the card himself. Or plans to. Then it wouldn't be much of a present, would it?"

"Ah," said Tom, wishing he had thought up some other story.

"Or maybe he threw the ticket away. Most of 'em do. Well, a third."

"That's it. He's not the type for pictures. I wanted this for his wife."

"Well, I've got the negs at home. What's he look like?"

Tom described Capstan, lovingly, in detail, and was delighted when the other said:

"I remember your mate. Bit of a comic? Thinks he's Charlie Chaplin? Yes. Gave me a magazine. God and that."

"He was passing out . . . ?"

"No no, just bunged it to me same as someone prob'ly bunged it to him. Charlie Chaplin."

"When you knock off for lunch could I go home with you and look through your negatives?"

"Why not? There'll be no mistake then. Not that I'd have any trouble. I remember the Gregory's bag he was carrying."

"The what?"

Two minutes later Tom was striding along the street. Capstan had been carrying the distinctive blue and black paper bag of Gregory's the gentlemen's outfitters. The snapshot, which the photographer had agreed to pick out himself, might not be needed. What most certainly would be needed was a good story; and Tom thought hard as he walked.

In front of Gregory's he stopped and looked through the window, looking deep inside beyond a decapitated model whose neck bled green silk. He felt immediately intimidated by the solemn interior. Which feeling he fought. This was no time for that kind of snob nonsense. He was a man with a mission. Besides, he was wearing a tie.

There were three departments inside. Suits, overcoats and slacks; headgear; shirts, underwear and accessories. Capstan's package was small enough to have been filled at either of the last two. Reasoning that a hat would not have been squashed under an arm, although a cap would, except that Capstan was not the cap type (he had, after all, been wearing a Panama), Tom decided on the third department.

He got his story and made it firm while waiting for the clerk to finish his present business. The customer at last coming out, Tom went in. He walked to the counter, shuffled himself affably and said, "Morning, young fella."

The salesman bowed, eyeing Tom's buttonless jacket. "Good day, sir."

"Listen." Tom flattened his hands on the counter and leaned forward. "I had a bit of an accident yesterday with my car. Farther up George Street there. I was in the right but the people in the other car say I was in the wrong. Are you with me?"

"Well—"

"Listen. There was one bloke walking by that really saw what happened and if—wait, I'll tell you what he looks like." After going through the description, including the Gregory's bag, Tom asked, "Sound familiar?"

"Yes, I recall the gentleman."

"Good lad. He saw what happened and I'd like to get hold of him and ask him to tell his version of the accident. Now you're with me, eh?"

The salesman nodded. "Perfectly, sir. The only thing is, will the gentleman care to do what you want? Will he care to get himself involved?"

"I don't see why not. It's the right and proper thing to do."

The salesman shook his head. "No, sir. I'm sure the gentleman will be quite annoyed by having to make a statement, see the police, appear before a magistrate, lose time and money, be bullied in the witness box by counsel. Quite annoyed, to say the least."

Tom gave a tutting sigh. His story didn't seem so good after all. The next moment, however, he was smiling, for the salesman said in a lowered voice, glancing around:

"So if you don't mention how you came by it, I'll go and get you the gentleman's name from his check."

Jack Partridge came out of the bathroom. He had washed, given his hair a superficial comb and, after brief thought, decided that a shave was not vital.

In the hall, with a furtive look at the kitchen door, he turned and went into the front lounge, an expansive modern room. Once through the door he crouched low, fingertips on the carpet, to circle round to the picture window. He peered out, searching every corner, doorway and tree.

This routine he had already been through a number of times the night before, every hour or so until seven, when he had at last fallen into a fitful sleep of bad dreams: scores of fleeting sketches from whose ugly silliness he fought himself away, to the rim of consciousness, only to sink into still another stupidity of blood and strange laughter.

Unlike the shadows which pained his imagination on previous visual scourings, he saw nothing now to give him worried pause. He rose slowly, tiredly, returned to the bedroom and began to finish dressing.

Because of daylight, no longer made aware of loneliness and insignificance by night, Jack felt the situation as a sigh's worth less intolerable. It was like standing under a massive chandelier that was bound to fall; watching it was bad, but, fear's scale always being topped by the unknown, the inability to watch it was impossible torture.

He would do no more considering of the circumstances, wondering when would the knock come on the door, trying to put himself in the place of the other man, seeing things from the angle of the police, preparing word for word the explanation to give Mildred, cataloguing the business and personal arrangements he should make while there was still time—all these he had been over countless times on his watch through the night. Enough was enough. For the present he would, as it were, tread water.

From sitting to put on his shoes, he rose. A dull pain ran through his head. It reminded him of his physical self, of the tingling ache in his eyes, the dryness of his throat and mouth, the weariness in his body. The only difference between this hangover and a real one was the cause; and the fact that time would not effect a cure.

Yet when Jack walked into the kitchen he was smiling. A brave attempt, he gave it up when his wife said, "You look awful."

"Do I? I feel all right though."

"Awful." Mildred Partridge pushed her sewing onto the table. "Sit here. You can have your temperature taken while I fix you some tucker."

Jack sat. He winced at the painful-sounding cracks of Mildred's wrist as she shook the thermometer, then allowed it to be thrust under his tongue. With the usual feeling of total imprisonment he sat immobile and gazed around the kitchen. He noted its sparkling cleanliness. Funny, he mused, how you took such things for granted.

He looked fondly at his wife. He remembered that last night when she came to bed, thinking him asleep, she had touched his brow, smoothed back his hair with a gentle hand and kissed him lightly on the cheek. At that moment he had been close to tears.

Silly, was his gruff thought. And silly to be feeling almost as bad now. He glared at the refrigerator, sat more erect, cleared his throat and told himself that he must not go completely to pieces. A grown man in tears. Silly.

Mildred returned and extracted the thermometer. "Hmm," she said, "no temperature." She sounded wistful.

63

"I told you, Mil. I feel good."

"I suppose it could have been that twenty-four hour flu."

"Yes, very likely. Yes, I'm sure that's what it was."

"But the twenty-four hours isn't up yet so perhaps you'd best stay in bed."

"I'm all right. Truly. Now what about that grub."

Back at the stove, Mildred explained that since it was noontime she was fixing him a good big brunch, every scrap of which he had to eat if he didn't want to make her cranky.

Jack smiled. Again the smile's life was brief. When the plate containing egg, ham, sausages, kidneys, potatoes, tomatoes and fried bread was put before him he felt sick.

"Okay?" asked Mildred proudly.

"Great," he said, lifting knife and fork.

She gave him no hope, sat down at the other side of the table and picked up her sewing. "Dig in."

To take his mind off what he was forcing himself to eat, Jack asked what she was making. She said, "Nothing. These are those shirts you bought. I got them out of the car."

"Shirts? Oh yes. Shirts."

"Not well made. I pulled one of the buttons and it came off. I'm stitching them all on good and strong."

"I see."

"You've got to look for things like that when you're buying clothes."

"Well, a woman knows about these things. A man just goes by appearance. You were right, Mil, I should've let you buy the shirts."

Mildred Partridge stayed her hands and raised her head slowly. She was too startled to feel any triumph, too startled to feel alarm. She looked at her husband of twenty-eight years, three months and some odd days until the shock

64

faded, when she told herself with regret that it was probably not a mellowing but the off-colourness which had prompted his acquiescence. And, she thought, he certainly did not look himself at all. Not that he looked awful either, despite her having told him so. With his hair tousled, his face pale, his tie not quite on centre, his eyes soft and, what was the word, vulnerable, yes, he . . .

"You know," she said abruptly, "you're a good-looking man, Jack."

Now Jack was startled. But no more than Mildred herself. She wished with dark fervour that she could take the foolish words back. Jack wished roughly the same.

They stared at one another helplessly. Next, they both began to blush.

Jack dived into his food, eating without nausea, even with eagerness, relieved at having some action to hide behind. Mildred stitched away rapidly. She swallowed a cry when the needle ran into her finger.

The telephone rang.

Almost in a shout, Mildred said, "I'll get it." She flung aside her sewing and went out to the hall.

Jack put down his knife and fork to think, to wonder what had made his wife be so outspoken. He got no further than repeating to himself her words, however, for he was brought suddenly and coldly to his fear by hearing:

"That's right. Jack Partridge.

"Well, he's here now as it happens. You can talk to him yourself.

"It doesn't matter, you say?

"Yes, I'm his wife.

"English? No.

"Yes, he did live there for a while. Years ago.

"Well, thirty years ago.

65

"Who is this, please?"

Jack rose to his feet with the tightness of an opening spring. One hand grabbed a lapel, the other became a fist and pressed against his mouth. The chandelier was falling.

"Yes," Mildred said, "that sounds like a pretty good description of Jack. He must be your old friend. I'll call him to the phone, eh? He'll be tickled pink."

Jack backed away to the outer door and put a hand behind him to fumble for the handle.

"Hello?

"Hello?

"Been disconnected."

Jack sagged, his hand dropping.

Mildred came into the kitchen. "Did you hear that? Funny, eh? This pommie wanted to know if you were the Jack Partridge he knew in London thirty-odd years ago. You must be, I said. He didn't give his name and then we got cut off. Who can it be, d'you think?"

Jack turned and opened the door. "God knows. I'm going to work."

"What if he rings back? He'll probably ring back any minute. What'll I say?"

"Tell him to come whenever he's ready."

The department store was crowded. People from offices and factories and those shops which closed for lunch augmented the regular shoppers and muddled in the aisles like sheep in loading runs.

Janet Tree, entering the store, was delighted. She had never before been out acquiring at this time of day and had

66

not realized how perfect it was. The crush made for cover. Being small, she was hardly seen at all. One was of course liable to get knocked about a bit. But it was worth while for safety. Henceforth she would come downtown only during the luncheon break.

She burrowed her way along to the camera counter. A camera she was determined to get. Apart from the value, she wanted to show Mr Beeker that her friends could take a hint. Although she had offered him cameras in the past, the occasions had been rare and the last one more than a year ago. What glory, she thought, if she could show up tomorrow at the pawnshop with the desired pair, a camera and a wristwatch.

Pressed about closely by shoppers she forged ahead. After passing with regret a display stack of boxed steak knives which seemed on the point of toppling over into the aisle, she came to a counter around which the people were standing two deep and above which glowed a mammoth transparent of the harbour bridge.

Janet wriggled through to the front. There were four salesgirls, each trying to be in three places at once. Janet noted with satisfaction that many in the crowd were handling the merchandise, examining cameras, tripods, meters and other mysteries of photography.

Before her, at chin level, poking above their token barrier of glass at the counter edge, were cameras the size of cigarette packs, all identical, all with a bewildering bristle of switches and buttons. She picked one up. Underneath it said *Made in Japan*. A ticket told the price as fifty dollars.

The origin gave her pause. After all, the Japs had been responsible for her husband's death. But then it occurred to her that this way they might not make any profit. She would be striking a tiny blow of retaliation. Also, fifty dollars was a large sum of money for a single acquisition.

She looked around. The salesgirls were glancing everywhere, glances too fleeting to see anything other than a blatant signal for attention. The people on either side were busy with their own considerations.

Janet lowered the camera and pushed it past the knitting set. Looking straight ahead she stood still and waited. Nothing happened. She was safe.

With a tremulous intake of breath she turned away and skirmished on.

In the book department she spent ten minutes, her browsing made pleasant by the fact that it was genuine. She even went so far as to consider buying, taking a fancy to a book on how to train a cocker spaniel—the pictures were most appealing.

Moving on she went to an escalator and rose to another floor. Here there were less people, the merchandise being on a monetarily larger scale or of more limited appeal—furniture, radionics, jewellery, watches. The counter of the last owned only one browsing couple and one assistant. Janet, having arrived there, made a slow circuit for effect and went back to the escalators. Her watch she would get from another store.

Downstairs, she had nearly reached the exit when it came to her that she was letting a good opportunity go by. The crowds were marvellous protection. Another day they might not be so dense. She should make hay. Take one more camera.

She turned back.

This time she chose a different side of the counter. She eased through the people and at first had to stand sideways.

After a while, the pressure slackening, she was able to face the rows of black and chrome gadgets.

Within reach was a camera similar to the one she had taken before, except that the dangling ticket said one hundred and twenty-three dollars. The price was rather frightening. This, Janet felt, was ridiculous. What had the price to do with accessibility? And accessibility was perfection itself.

She reached out, lifted the camera and brought it to her chest. From the tops of her eyes, head down, she looked at the salesgirls. They did not return the look. She lowered her hands preliminary to the final drop.

Another glance at the staff. Still safe.

About to lower the camera into her bag, something made her jell to a stop. The something was a sensation, like that of being stared at on the nape of the neck. Her armpits prickled. Her heart began a tap tap tap.

Slowly she looked up. The salesgirls were not watching. What was wrong, she realized, though with no relaxation in tension, was that now she was almost alone. Lunchtime was over: the crowd had thinned.

Taking a chance she knew to be wrong, she plunged the camera into her bag. She turned. She began to walk. Her legs were oddly stiff. The thinly populated aisle appeared to stretch an alarmingly endless way to the exit. She looked down, as a climber looks up.

The abrogation of distance decreased her alarm while allowing her tension to grow. The original feeling was stronger. She knew that she should lift her head, if not to see if she were being watched by someone to at least appear as though she were behaving in a normal way. Her head stayed lowered.

She was nearly at the door. She could see the feet of the people walking past outside. She longed to race the last few

69

yards. She felt if she couldn't race she would have to scream.

The voice which pulled her to a petrified halt could have been directed at anybody. But Janet knew that she was the one accused; and there was nothing but accusation in the:

"Excuse me, madame."

She swayed. A hand took a firm grip on her elbow. Her senses undulated, her heart thumped and she felt she was going to faint.

The voice, male, was saying something unintelligible. She tried to concentrate. She was able to do so by the letting go of her tension and the admission of capture.

Slack mouthed, she raised her head. She saw towering above her a red face with hair and bushy moustache of speckled grey. Rather a nice face, she thought sadly.

She whispered, "I beg your pardon?"

"I said I'd like you to come to the office for a minute."

She asked why, dreamily and horribly conscious of being the centre of attention. All around, most movement had stopped; most, not all; some people were still getting better positions, those near stepping back, those far stepping in. Janet groped a hand inside her coat and clutched through her clothing at the front safety pin.

The man had been speaking again. His drone ended now with, "Understand?"

She shook her head.

"I think you do, madame. Come along."

She found herself being walked back down the aisle. Watching dazedly the people as they moved out of the way, she told herself that this could not really be happening. How could Mrs Janet Tree of Dimple Hill be disgraced? God didn't let such things happen to decent, respectable people.

A door, an office, a desk, a chair. She was made to sit. A

new voice asked for her name and address. She made no answer. What would the neighbours say when they read about it in the papers? She shrank down in her seat.

"Madame!" said the new voice sharply.

They kept saying madame, she thought with a hint of sick amusement. How ridiculous.

"Shall I send for the police before I ask for an explanation?"

Was there hope? She sat up, saying, "Janet Tree, West Wind, Gormon Lane, Dimple Hill."

At the other side of the desk sat a thin man whose top lip lay ineffectually above two large protruding teeth. He wore spectacles with frames of a vicious thickness and blackness. By the desk end stood the man with the bushy moustache, looking down at her shopping bag, beside which were the two cameras. He depressed the knitting needles and wool with a forefinger. "Cute, that is," he said.

No, there was no hope.

"I'm Johnson," said the second man, "the manager here." He opened and began to thumb through a telephone directory. "Janet Tree, eh? Well, if you're speaking the truth you should know your telephone number."

Janet gave her number. Johnson found a place in the book and nodded. "All right, Mrs Tree. We've got that established. Now perhaps you'd like to tell me how long you've been stealing from us."

Janet shook her head in despair. The bushy moustache man said, "Oh, she hasn't *stolen* anything, Mr Johnson. *Honestly*. She had every intention of paying. Just slipped her mind, that's all."

"Mrs Tree?"

"I didn't know what I was doing," Janet whimpered. "Please may I go home now?"

"Kleptomania," said bushy moustache. "That's what it was. Couldn't help yourself, could you?"

Mr Johnson looked at him with eyebrows raising above his spectacles. "Police?"

"Absolutely, sir. It's the only way. These people'll rob you blind. Why, there's over a hundred and seventy dollars' worth of stuff here. You can't let her get away with it."

"What if they refuse to prosecute? It's happened before. They don't like these cases. They say the way we display goods we're asking to be robbed and they're not going to spend time on our mistakes."

"I know, sir. But this is a bit much. A hundred and seventy isn't a box of chocolates. If she's got a record they'll be glad to prosecute—"

"I haven't," said Janet quickly. "I've never been in trouble."

"—and if she hasn't," the man went on, "I'll sign the charge myself."

With a glum nod, Johnson reached for the telephone.

"Er," said Janet.

"Yes?"

Bushy moustache: "Now comes the pleading bit. They're all the same."

"Yes, Mrs Tree?"

Janet leaned forward. "It's the Japanese," she said. "They killed my husband in the war."

"What?"

"I'm a war-widow. I get a pension. Every Japanese thing I can get hold of I fix so they don't benefit. Like these cameras. They wouldn't get any profit from these, would they?"

"They already have. We buy, not steal."

"Oh. I didn't know."

72

"But what were you going to do with them?"

"I was going to cross the harbour bridge and throw them over the side."

"Pretty neat story," said bushy moustache, lifting one of the cameras. "Only this one's from Germany."

"Oh. I didn't know that either. I thought they were all Japanese."

Johnson: "Your husband was killed in the war?"

"New Guinea," said Janet, and as a fillip added, "They tortured him."

The man with the moustache groaned softly. Mr Johnson sighed. They exchanged looks, Janet following birdlike every nuance of eyebrow and mouth. Again she offered, as though it were the answer to everything, "I get a pension."

Johnson looked at Janet and folded his arms. He said, his voice quietly cold, "Your name and description will be circulated through all stores. If you ever do any more stealing it had better be well away from this area. You may go. And if I should find out that you've been lying to me I'll have you arrested. You may go."

Janet rose, sat again when her legs gave way, began to cry softly and whispered, "Could you get me a taxi, please."

On a main suburban artery stood the garage called Partridge (Pty) Ltd. Flat-topped, white-painted, it was a long low building with a stretch of plate glass between the end service doors through which could be seen half a dozen cars—clean, sound, one-owner, terms arranged. The forecourt was a service station.

Jack Partridge got out of his car on the side parking lot. Returning with grave nods, not attempting to act, the greetings of various employees, he went into the clanging workshop and threaded through the invalid vehicles to a corner. He climbed a stairway and entered his cramped office, which smelt of warm wood. Closing the door on the noise he sat at his desk.

The telephone call Mildred had taken, that was what he thought about. They were checking, he supposed. As expected, it had not taken them long to find his name and address. What they were waiting for now he couldn't guess. But perhaps they were already at the house, or on their way here.

The telephone by his elbow gave its shrill cry. His body jumped. He stood up, tugged down his jacket, licked his lips and lifted the receiver.

A voice said, "Just saw you come in, Mr Partridge. It's about the appraisal on that Chev trade-in. Could we go five hundred?"

Jack took a deep breath. "Use your own judgement," he said. "And don't bother me again, please. I'm busy." He dropped the receiver into its cradle and sat.

From a drawer he brought a bottle and a glass, both coated with dust. He wiped out the glass with his handkerchief and poured a small measure of whisky. He sipped, shuddered, put down the drink and leaned back.

What, he mused, would his reaction be when the police did come. Well, he would say he was Jack Partridge and claim to not know what they were talking about, and stick to that. In time, with the identification and the fingerprints from the flat, they would get a conviction. He would never confess. How could he? Confess to what? No one would understand. Justice did not mean justice in the purest sense, it meant applying rules with admitted flaws to set types of crimes. Here there was no crime.

74

Carlotta. They didn't know what she was like. No one could know. No one knew anyone outside the walls of an intimate relationship. The charming man could be a vicious bastard at home, the sweet little woman a snarling bitch.

Bitch, *le mot juste*. Although, naturally, he had not been able to see it at first. Not that he was dazzled either. He found her attractive, nothing more.

Carlotta was tall and slim, tending to be skinny, no breasts to speak of. Her black hair she wore shoulder length, permed to waves, and was incessantly pushing it back from her face with long fingers with long, crimson fingernails. Her dark eyes were large and expectant, her best feature, her mouth was small and coy, as though she had just drawn it in to keep from smiling, her jaw-line was good and her nose was long. Her nose was overlong. Worse, it had an articulated tip. Formed like miniscule buttocks, the tip jiggled as she talked. A disturbing and ultimately annoying thing to watch. He never became completely reconciled to her nose. Even when he thought himself in love he didn't care to look at her while she was talking. But that came later.

They met at a supper dance in Brighton. She was with a man, he with a girl. The couples got into conversation at the bar and decided to share a table. Carlotta talked a lot and drank a lot, as did her friend. Jack and his girl, a casual date, confided to one another while dancing that the strangers were a little fast, like most Londoners.

Carlotta asked Jack for a dance. He blushed and said yes. When they were on the floor, Carlotta asked with a smile: "Are you people down here for a dirty weekend too?"

Jack mumbled that no, he lived near Brighton, and began to talk about the band. He was shocked and embarrassed. He decided to cut the evening short. For one thing, he found Carlotta disturbing in a way he did not understand, for another he was having to buy round for round with the man and already had spent more than he could afford for drinks he didn't want. After a polite exchange of addresses and telephone numbers, Jack left and took his girl home. He never expected to see Carlotta again.

At that time he was living on a smallholding with his widowed mother. A tenant farmer, he had worked hard for eight years at a job he disliked, having been forced to give up his plan of going to University when his father died. His vocation, engineering, he followed in the only way possible, by playing attendance on the farm machinery and his two-seater Sunbeam.

Three months after the meeting with Carlotta, Jack's mother also died. He was alone and free. He gave up the tenancy, sold everything saleable and drove to London, where he got a cheap room until he could find a job and establish himself.

Jobs, however, were hard to come by in the Thirties. He became one of London's half million unemployed, with the extra disadvantage of an unfinished education.

It was only when his money shrank piteously low that he thought of the couple he had met in Brighton. The man had mentioned something about being the manager of a factory. From among his papers Jack sifted out Carlotta's number and rang her up, as if being social—he would get around to jobs later. After reminding her of their meeting he said:

"But I don't suppose you remember me."

"Of course I do. You're the boy with the blush. Come for a drink at six."

Carlotta had a flat in a luxury block. To Jack it was like something straight out of Hollywood. She was an excellent

76

hostess, soon had her guest relaxed and talking about himself, the events which had brought him to London and what he hoped to achieve. She acted as naturally as if they had known each other for days on an ocean liner.

Jack was impressed. He thought her enormously sophisticated. He also thought that he must appear to be a country bumpkin. In fact, after his third drink he heard himself ask her if this was not so.

"Of course not, darling," she said. "I think you're perfectly sweet. Manly. And very handsome."

Again he was shocked. The women he knew never said such things. He drained his glass in protest against his feelings, which he was convinced were wrong, parochial.

Carlotta said, "If you are a mite countrified you have the glow of youth to carry it off."

They talked about ages and how they didn't matter. He was twenty-six, she thirty. Jack considered her one of the most intelligent and attractive women he had ever met.

They had more drinks. Things became hazy. There was a walk, a meal in a restaurant, a visit to a pub for more drinks. The last thing Jack remembered was singing in a taxi.

When he awoke it was morning and he knew by the clean white ceiling above the bed that he was not in his digs. He turned his head. He was lying beside Carlotta. She, raised on one elbow, her upper body bare, was watching him closely. Any feeling of shock which he might have had was unable to get through to the still-deadened senses.

While not a virgin, Jack had never been in bed with a woman before, his previous victories having been scored over protest in fields and barns, all fumblings in the dark, and he wondered: what now? Was the path clear to sex, or had he been allowed to sleep here merely out of good fellowship? After all, Carlotta was so worldly she might think nothing of the strictly platonic sharing of a bed.

Bold in his alcohol, however, and urged on by desire, he said, "Let's make love."

She came into his arms fast. "Again? Oh, you lovely man."

That afternoon Jack moved into Carlotta's flat. She said she would help him find a job, though not with her boy friend of the time in Brighton, with whom she was no longer on speaking terms. Meanwhile, he was to be her guest. Jack told himself that the arrangement was perfect, that he would pay back her generosity as soon as he started to earn.

Yet somehow they never had time for job hunting. There was so much to do. After a late night, and every night was late, it was eleven before they got up, and eleven was pink gin time. Then came a drink or two out, lunch with wine, a siesta, cocktails at friends' places or one of the thousand lounge-bars where Carlotta was known, dinner, a party, a club, nightcaps at home, bed.

There were of course variations on this standard theme. Sometimes they stayed in bed all day. Sometimes they stayed out all night. Once in a while in the early hours they went to look at the tramps sleeping underneath the arches or along the Embankment because Carlotta always found them amusing. Also they went racing, rally driving, boating; they saw dramas, ballet, boxing; they listened to plays, poetry readings, concerts and Carlotta's friends telling them what a wonderful couple they made and how two could permanently live as cheaply as one.

Jack was continually being shocked by his mistress. At her jokes, her language, the acts carnal she requested and offered, her easy switch from smile to sneer, her rages. Even more shocked at the things she confided or shouted when she was drunk and refuted when sober: that she had not, as she had said, been a model, but a call girl, of the highest type, mind . . . that she had sold her virginity for two hundred pounds at the age of sixteen . . . that she had spent more on abortions than some people spend on educating their children . . . that in case he didn't know it he was a pimp . . . that once she had blinded in one eye a man she disliked by stabbing him with his own cigar . . . that only idiots obeyed the law . . . that some of the fights they had she provoked for the sheer pleasure of fighting.

Physical and verbal, public and private, their fights were frequent. Jack slapped Carlotta at a party and tugged her hair on the King's Road. Carlotta abused Jack loudly from the buying of a ticket on the tote until their dog ran a slavering second. Jack twisted Carlotta's arm on the upper level of a number twelve bus. Carlotta kicked Jack twice in a taxi, once again at the door of their flat and several times more when they got inside. Jack roared vituperation at Carlotta in W.C.I. In a club, Carlotta slowly and gracefully poured a glass of champagne over Jack's head. Jack threw his shoes at Carlotta, she retaliated with everything she could lift.

Jack was violently in love and filled with hatred, a hate tempered by the fact that he was never sure when Carlotta was being serious.

The reasons for their fighting were if he looked too long at another woman or commented favourably on another woman's dress, the time his car had a flat tyre, not lighting her cigarette fast enough, being unenthusiastic at receiving from her the presents of clothing, his objection to being called a country clod, when he found her passport and learned that she was thirty-five, when she came home after being away for hours and refused to say where she had been, the times in restaurant or bar that instead of slipping

79

him money on the sly she made an open and ostentatious display of being the paymaster, when he said he'd had enough to drink and wanted to go home, when it rained.

With their almost permanent togetherness and the emotion bred by familiarity, with Jack's continued workless state and feeling of uselessness, their arguments grew more habitual. There came an equal balance between periods of undying love and unquenchable hatred.

Their biggest fight took place in the flat. Jokingly he mentioned one of her drunken confidences, that her real name was Lottie. The battle was on, she screeching vile epithets, he trying to be calm and logical, until the names became too much and he began a roaring repetition of "Lottie!" Since there was nothing to throw she flew at him with her fingernails and raked his face.

Spurting blood, he picked up a paper knife.

She screamed, "Remember who you are!"

He paused. He remembered that he was a well brought up young man, a liberal and a decent type. He put down the knife and left the flat and again thought he had seen the last of Carlotta.

Jack realized he was standing. He sat down. His wet palms he wiped on his trousers.

That, he thought, had been a close thing. Too close. Hatred compounded by the instinct for self-preservation. He had been able to stop himself, but it had been close.

He looked at his glass of whisky, wrinkled his nose, splashed the liquid onto the board floor and put away bottle and glass. Slumping down, he recalled with dismay the incredible bitchiness of Carlotta, and with amazement the extent to which he had let himself get involved and sink to a disgusting level.

After a while he realized that he was uncomfortable. Not only was his chair far from being the type for lounging in, his office was too small: he felt confined, hemmed.

He got up, opened the door and stepped out onto the landing. He halted abruptly. He eased himself back through the doorway. Near Reception, talking to the works manager, was the man from George Street.

"Good-o, sir. If you bring it in tomorrow I'll get them on it straight away."

"What will the charge be, d'you think?" asked Tom Brady, enjoying his role of a prospective repairs customer and unwilling to let it go.

"Between twenty and thirty dollars, I reckon. Now if you'll excuse me, sir? Good day."

Outside, walking, Tom thought that he had done very well. Since getting the name at Gregory's he had accomplished quite a lot. Both business and home addresses had been given in the telephone directory. A call to the house had established that Jack Partridge and Peter Capstan were certainly one and the same. At the garage, choosing that first for a visit because Partridge was at home, he had talked to a youth on the petrol pumps and the works manager, with skillful questions filling himself in on the proprietor: family, business, kind of person—a bit of a tyrant, it seemed, but straight as a die. Oh sure.

Tom thought himself quite a detective (the London force would never know what it had missed in ignoring his capabilities). The way he had found out about Gregory's and then tricked the salesman there into giving away the customer's name had been investigation of the highest order.

And he was being methodical, writing everything down in a notebook he had bought for that purpose. It had cost twenty cents, and attached, in a pouch, was a pencil.

When he stopped at a bus stop to begin the trip to Dimple Hill, Tom took out his book for the enjoyment of the act, slid free the pencil and made a ponderous notation.

In comparison to her rigid bedroom, Janet Tree's parlour was the middle word in comfort. Compared to other parlours, it was rigid.

There was too much furniture and too little sloppiness. A pleasing free-form note was the canary in a cage in the bay window; the small yellow bird, giving reproachful chirps, bounded and fluttered from perch to swing, not as if in protest against captivity but the lack of life everywhere else in its world.

Janet lay on the couch, a dampened cloth on her brow, picture perfect as an Edwardian lady with the vapours. Having recovered from the shock of her near arrest, she was now sunk in the gloom of reaction.

Her acquiring career, she mused, was in jeopardy. Downtown Sydney was out for ever. She would have to go to suburban shopping districts, which would naturally be smaller, therefore with fewer people, therefore more dangerous. The only safe solution was another city, meaning trips away from home of two and three days duration. And what would her gentlemen do for breakfast? They would surely leave. But what would be, would have to be. She could not give up acquiring. She had to have the money. She could not and would not go back to her old nervousness and irritability.

With a gesture of despair which had in it also an accusation of deficiency, Janet flung aside the damp cloth. She got off the couch and went into her kitchen to make some tea. The cup that cheers, did not. She felt more miserable than ever, thinking of the little culinary luxuries on which she would have to skimp—butter for frying in, smoked salmon, fresh cream—in order to afford the luxury absolute.

She looked around the kitchen, the parlour and her bedroom, picking out the pawnable or saleable items. There were not many. In any case, she thought, that was only putting off the day of non-reckoning. While in the bedroom she looked at her savings book and bank account. Small assurance there. If only she had been less extravagant in the past!

A job? she wondered. Doing what? She had no qualifications and was getting along in years. Sell the house and move into a rented flat? Never.

She gave it up, went back to the couch and the damp cloth.

At four o'clock the doorbell rang. Janet shot upright. She told herself to calm down, calm down, got up and went to the front door and eased it open.

A large man, fatly smiling. Janet's twinge of nervousness at the former was allayed by the latter. "Good afternoon," she said.

"Mrs Tree?" asked Tom Brady.

"Yes."

"My name's Brady, ma'am. A lady down the street tells me you rent rooms."

"Ah," said Janet, nodding slowly. She went on nodding as she thought with a perk in spirits that here was a gift from heaven: the answer. If she rented her two top rooms and made, say, a monthly two-day trip to another city, she might yet be able to manage.

Tom wondered if there were something wrong with the woman. All she could do was nod. He coughed.

"Sorry," Janet said. "I was, er, considering. I haven't been taking any more gentlemen guests lately, but I might just start doing so." Her use of the word *gentleman* caused Janet to pay closer attention to her caller. His face, hair and clothes made her realize that what she had said was quite misapropos. She told herself, however, that he looked as respectable as a yeoman could, and that a client was a client, and that being middle-aged he would no doubt be terribly quiet.

Tom coughed again. The woman had stopped nodding, true, but now she was looking at him as though he were something hanging from a hook in a butcher's. He was beginning to consider the idea of leaving when Mrs Tree said:

"Would you like to see the room, Mr . . . ?"

"Brady. Well, all right."

They went up one flight of stairs, then another, Tom staring with apprehension, the rent in mind, at the quality of the furnishings, Janet chattering about how the view from above compensated for the two flights.

They entered a front room. Tom walked at once to the bay window and looked out through the lace curtain. The view, while good, was not the view he wanted; it was blocked by another bay some two yards distant. He asked:

"How about that next room? Could I change with the lodger there?"

Suppressing a moue at his choice of words, Janet said, "It's empty. By accident, you understand. The occupant moved out yesterday."

84

They went next door. The view was perfect. Tom could see the Partridge residence in every detail and its every approach. He was close enough to pick out the buttons on the dress of the small girl who was sitting on the front lawn.

He turned to examine the room. There was a massive double bed, a wardrobe that leaned nastily outward from the wall, an ochre Indian carpet, an engraving of the Tay Bridge collapsing and in the middle of the room a seating ensemble: low table sided by a sprawling armchair and a straight chair, looking like the tête-à-tête of a fat voluptuary and a terrified miss sitting Christianly upright with legs firmly, protectively together.

Tom asked for and was given the terms. Not only was the rent twice what he had been paying, it was not for full board, breakfast only. It was out of the question. He couldn't possibly afford such a rent.

"I'll take it," he said.

Downstairs, learning with pleasure that Mr Brady wished to move in at once, as soon as he had brought his things, Janet wrote out a receipt and collected a week's money. Warm and responsive now, she asked her new gentleman about himself. He said he was from Britain originally and Janet said what a coincidence, her grandmother had been from Britain, which in Australia is as much a coincidence as two strangers discovering that each, as children, had been to school.

"And are you working around here, Mr Brady?"

"Actually, I'm retired," Tom said, looking closely at Mrs Tree, alert for the usual reaction. "I used to be on the police force."

The reaction was far greater than he had expected. The woman turned pale even as he watched. One hand groped for her stomach, as if she were going to be sick. Again he feared for the state of her mind. But he told himself she was most likely one of those people who were over-impressionable.

"Well, I'll get off and pack my bag," he said. "See you soon."

Janet stared at the door when it had closed behind Mr Brady. An ex-policeman, she thought in dread. It had been obvious right from the start, yet greed had made her ignore the signs. She was being investigated, here in her own home. And he didn't mind if she knew—that hard, searching look in his eyes when he had answered her question. He would check on her past and trip her up in conversations. They would find out about Mr Beeker. She would be ruined.

Tottering, Janet made her broken way back to the parlour.

At five o'clock Jack Partridge turned his car into Gormon Lane. His solemnity was shattered by a smile as he saw, farther along, the small figure of his granddaughter. He put on speed.

The girl was five years old, plump and plain. When Jack swung into the drive she jumped up from the lawn to wave and caper: then chase the car up to the garage.

Jack alighted, stopped his grandchild's charge, lifted her and threw her in the air. They laughed at one another. Jack cuddled her close; closer than normal; so close that the girl squeaked a complaint. Jack put a smile back on his face and they went into the kitchen.

"Sit down," Mildred said, sliding a plate on the table. "I've made you just sandwiches for tea because I want to take Pam back home."

"Good."

"It isn't good really. You know you didn't finish your brunch."

"I ate something out."

"And that man didn't ring back after all."

"Not important," said Jack. He sat at the table with his grandchild and showed an attentive face to what she was saying while thinking about that man. The situation was no clearer. After talking with his works manager, as if idly, Jack had learned nothing about the prospective customer other than he had seemed to be inordinately curious about the garage's boss.

"Are you eating?" called Mildred.

Jack dutifully bit into a sandwich. Finding himself hungry, he ate with interest, dipping his bread into the Worcestershire sauce which he flooded onto the plate.

His thoughts were returning to their former topic when he was brought up short by a word of the child's. "What?" he said.

She pouted. "You're not listening."

"Yes, I am. Questions, you said."

"Yes, a man. At the front of the house."

Jack glanced toward his wife. She was taking no notice. He asked, "What colour sweater was he wearing?"

Promptly the girl answered, "Green."

"That's right. A big man, eh?"

"Oh yes. With a little bit of white hair."

Jack's appetite died. He forced the sandwich down for the sake of harmony and asked, "What kind of questions were they, darling?"

Nice ones, the girl said, about how old she was and how many sisters and brothers and cousins she had and what was her favourite ice cream. He was a nice man.

"He didn't ask about me?"

"Yes. A funny question."

"What?"

87

"He asked if you was cruel."

Mildred came to the table, took her husband's plate to the sink and said, "I've just got to wash up these things and then I'll get off with Pam. Her mother'll be getting worried." She nearly dropped the plate when she heard Jack say: "I'll help you dry, if you like."

Mildred turned on him a worried look. But Jack was not noticing. He was gazing out of the window at the sky as if he had never seen a sky before.

4

During the following days there was a high degree of watchfulness and snooping in the confines of Gormon Lane. Jack Partridge was watched by his fretful wife, and by Tom Brady, who was watched by Janet Tree and also, coming full circle, by Jack Partridge.

Jack had soon discovered the fact of Tom's residence in the street. That same evening, after sitting with determination near the front room window for an hour, he had been rewarded by seeing Tom Brady walk casually past, giving the house a less than casual scrutiny, continue on up the street and enter Mrs Tree's. A telephone call to Mr Snow, the divinity student, whom Jack knew through his connexion with the local church, a call supposedly relating to a church bazaar, had elicited in passing that "West Wind" had a new boarder called Tom Brady. In addition to the satisfaction of at last being able to put a name to the face, Jack felt, oddly enough, reassured by Brady's presence. He had the chandelier firmly in view.

Janet Tree felt more or less the same, after recovering from the shock of her assumption as to her new gentleman's motives. At least, she thought, she could keep an eye on him and possibly prevent any progress in his investigation, pump to find out how much he knew and at the same time do everything she could to get him on her side. In fact, despite her fear, Janet found the situation exciting, even romantic. There was an atmosphere of electricity in the house.

Mildred Partridge became worried and tense as she waited for the next sign of sickness—an offer of help, a kind word—for sickness she had decided it must be. She watched Jack surreptitiously, his actions, his speech. There was a definite change in the man. When one afternoon he brought her a bunch of flowers she became dizzy and only with a great exertion of will prevented herself from asking him to seek medical help; instead, she lay down in a darkened room for half an hour.

Tom Brady was having a grand time the whiles. He sat at his observation post in the bay window watching Partridge's comings and goings and making scribbles in his notebook, on the first page of which he had glued the snapshot given him by his photographer friend. Why he did all this he didn't stop to wonder, he simply enjoyed the doing, which enjoyment was not a whit diminished by the knowledge that Jack Partridge was perfectly aware of what was taking place. Had the reverse been true, he would have been rather disappointed.

To Tom the world was bright and shiny. Never had he felt better. Nor had he ever been paid so much attention, been so coddled. A truly magnificent breakfast was delivered to his door promptly at eight, his laundry was returned milk white, when he asked if he might borrow an iron to press his trousers Mrs Tree insisted on pressing them herself. She often stopped him on midstair to chat, and once invited him into her parlour for afternoon tea, when they had a delightful conversation about department stores. Tom reacted to the attentions of what he thought of as this young and pretty thing by putting on a lordly mien. But he was flattered to an immense grade and couldn't help wondering if she were not overstepping the bounds of commercial hospitality. On his third day at "West Wind" he bought a toothbrush.

Janet Tree found soon that she actually liked Tom Brady. He had presence, a certain air of determination and self-confidence and purpose, altogether an invigourating person to have about the house. When the undertaker's assistant, Mr East, came to complain to her of the snoring from the room above his she surprised both herself and Mr East by replying with some heat that there was nothing wrong with snoring, it was manly to snore. She apologized later and said she would speak to Mr Brady. Still . . .

As the days passed, Jack Partridge settled into a state of nerveless lethargy, a faintly melancholy yet not unhappy sense of twilight. He knew his time was limited. Unconcerned by the fact that Tom Brady was trailing somewhere behind, he took himself for long walks, seeing things to which he had long been blinded by familiarity. He wrote letters to people he had not thought of in years. He got from the local library books he had always wanted to read but had never had time for. He enjoyed sitting on his lawn and doing nothing other than listen to the birds and occasionally pick up and crush in his hand a eucalyptus leaf to savour its perfume. He visited more often his sons and their families. He took all his grandchildren on a picnic, a panic he would formerly not have countenanced, and came through the ordeal with calmness. His patience had no end.

One evening he asked his wife would she like to go out for dinner. This was too much for Mildred. Gulping into tears, she begged him to see a doctor. He replied, thinking fast, that he had done so that morning because he too had been worried about his health; he was worried no longer; he was in fine condition. They went to dinner. They split a bottle of champagne and laughed like teenagers, until they got home and into bed. Then came a sudden, disturbing silence. Jack took Mildred in his arms. Or Mildred took Jack in her arms. It was difficult to tell. They made love, not with the hearty camaraderie of the past but with a sad tenderness which made them wonder afterwards as they lay unsleeping in the dark how it was they knew so little about each other and themselves.

Janet Tree came into her parlour and glanced in the mantel mirror for a final look. She was dressed up. On her hair was a pill-box hat, emerald green to match her best coat and her clip-on earrings. With its features made prominent by a layer of cosmetics, her face had more of a simian cast than ever. The canary in the cage ruffled every feather in a troubled sort of way.

Janet was satisfied, thought she looked quite the type to patronize Sydney's most expensive shops as a cash customer.

There was a tap on the door. "Come in," called Janet cheerfully, her mind on the approaching treat.

Mr East entered, bowed his mane of dark hair with white trimmings and said, "I'm afraid it's about Mr Brady again."

"Oh dear. I did ask him to try and sleep on his side."

"Well, he isn't, Mrs Tree. And if that weren't bad enough, the walking's getting on my nerves now."

"The walking?"

"Yes," said Mr East, squinting indignantly beyond his nose, made brave by not having been attacked for complaining. "Practically every evening he walks. In and out of the bay. It wouldn't be so bad if it were regular pacing. It isn't.

It might be one minute before he walks, it might be five or it might be fifteen." Mr East's voice rose an octave: "It's the waiting, Mrs Tree! The tension!"

"Oh dear."

The undertaker's assistant calmed himself with a staggered exhalation of breath. "I can't concentrate on anything, really I can't."

"I'll speak to him, Mr East."

"I hope so," he said, turning to the door. "Thank you." Before going out he added in a distant voice, as if talking to himself, "I don't really want to leave here."

Janet sighed. It was, she reasoned, most distracting to have someone walking about in the room above. Mr East was not to be blamed for his complaint. But what could she do? She had dropped a heavy hint about the snoring. Any more hints might tend to antagonize. Which was unthinkable. Mr Brady must not be urged on in his investigation by personal animosity.

Janet paused for a moment. Except, she mused further, that there seemed not to be an investigation. He never asked questions, never snooped around, never talked to the other boarders, never followed her when she went out. The only solution must be that he was playing a waiting game. So what was he waiting for?

Shrugging, Janet decided that whatever method Mr Brady used to collect evidence, and she might try to find out by adroit questioning, until he showed his hand she would continue her plan of appeasement.

She lifted the telephone, dialled and told the voice at the far end, speaking in grander tones than normal, "Mrs Tree of West Wind, Gormon Lane, would like a taxi at once, please."

She walked into the bay to wait, making soothing sounds

at her canary until the taxi appeared. Outside, at the kerb, she nodded when asked by the cabbie if she were Mrs Tree, then stood still. After a moment the man turned and looked at her curiously. Janet looked at the rear door. Tutting, the man hauled himself out, opened the door and ushered Janet inside with a mock ceremony which she ignored. Whatever his attitude, this one was one of the details that added up to the total joy and she was not going to be cheated.

Fifteen minutes later the taxi turned off the bustle of George Street into a quiet thoroughfare lined with shops whose character was clear in their facades' successful blending of opulence with the sedate. Dismissing the taxi here, into one of these shops went Janet, into an ambience of respect, money, quality, money, perfume, money, soft music and money. Already she could feel a tingle of the impending thrill.

It was a large room with a low ceiling to make it more intimate. On stands which crouched superiorly distant from one another were leather goods, crystal, monolithic pieces of china, furs, and other objects not so much of art as of expensive living.

There were three or four customers, three or four salespeople—the latter keeping in the background until required. Here you were not pressed or even gently persuaded; when you needed attention you beckoned, preferably without seeming to do so.

Janet wandered slowly around the stands. She fingered a length of cloth, stroked a hide surface, chimed her fingernails against a glitter of cut glass. These actions, together with the large sums murmured by diminutive tickets, changed Janet's inner tingling to a glow, a warmth which had its seat between the pit of her stomach and her spine.

She lifted a stole, admired it at arm's length. A blueish

grey, soft as cotton wool, it was shot through with metallic glints. She brought it to her and stroked it gently.

A breathless glance at the ticket showed her that her choice was right. One hundred and fifty dollars, all but a few cents. Expensive and useless.

The glow inside growing, spreading, she walked at a slow dreamy pace to one of the inobtrusive cash desks. There she was met by a young man, dark suit, silver tie, who said softly:

"That is rather an attractive stole, isn't it, madame?"

"Gorgeous."

"Angora wool, cashmere, gold thread."

Janet gave a happy nod, whispering, "I'll take it."

The stole was lifted tenderly from her arms and folded for wrapping. Janet watched, eyes fixed, body tense. Her chest rose and fell quickly. The glow had spread to reach from her breasts to her knees. She cuddled clasped hands against her throat.

The stole was wrapped, the receipt made out. "One forty-nine seventy-five, please, madame."

Janet stepped to the desk and fumbled money from her bag, letting it fall where it would. The salesman took a share, returned the rest, which Janet put away with only a vague awareness of the act: the glow was rising to envelope her lungs. She leaned on the desk. Her knees dithered against one another. She gasped as the glow and her breathing reached a crescendo with the contraction of lower muscles—the salesman was coming; with the change.

Janet's lean on the desk became a sag. She felt released, as if from pain. She would have enjoyed a soft, cheerful weep. Blurredly she was aware of the salesman passing her a coin and of his voice asking if she were feeling all right.

She nodded, drew a long breath, smiled and said, "Yes."

The salesman saw Janet to the door and outside. She walked to the corner. She felt weak and dizzy, but also cozy, relaxed and happy. She was unable to keep the smile from her face.

Finding at the corner that George Street's blare and push was too alien to her present mood, she went back. For a quarter hour she traversed streets of comparative calm, hugging her purchase and her pleasure.

As her dreamy state diminished, she became increasingly conscious of the crinkly package in her arms. Its bulk was awkward. And what was she going to do with the stole? She couldn't possibly ever wear such a thing. And Mr Beeker wouldn't buy. No clothing, that was a firm rule.

She walked a while longer, clinging to the remnants of the first flush of pleasure, whose qualities, she knew, would last for days; and when it was time to think about going home she slipped into an alley, dropped her package onto a collection of refuse and garbage cans, turned and hurried away.

Jack Partridge got up and switched off the television set while his wife went to open the blinds. Mildred said, "That wasn't bad, now was it?"

"No," said Jack, truthfully. "Not bad at all." He had been surprised to find the travel programme so interesting.

"There are some things worth watching on the box."

"Of course there are."

"And you," she said, "always saying what a load of bull it was."

"Jealousy."

"Eh?"

"I thought you might elope with a television set."

Mildred snorted with derision and pleasure as she left the room. Jack followed her into the kitchen. "How about a drive?"

"Me? I've got the baking to do."

"Then I'll take myself out in the fresh air." Jack had an urge to go downtown. As yet he didn't know why. "Maybe we'll have a drive tomorrow."

"Sunday. We'll be going to church."

"We will?"

"We didn't go last week, remember? So tomorrow."

Jack turned at the door. "No, I won't be going. You can though."

"Not without you," said Mildred, pulling packets from a cupboard. "Why aren't you going tomorrow?"

"It's not only tomorrow. I don't think I'll be going again."

She looked around. "Why?"

"Well, I don't really believe in all that stuff, you know."

Blinking, Mildred slowly straightened. "You . . . ?"

Jack said a fast, "See you later." He went outside and strode to his car.

Getting in, he told himself with annoyance that he would have to get out of the habit of saying and doing things which startled his wife. She would get the idea again that he was sick.

As he reversed onto the road, however, Jack congratulated himself on his decision. It was time he stopped being a hypocrite. And perhaps his reasons for going in the first place had not been quite as grand as he had supposed. The church, its very smell, had always evoked a halcyon area of his past and he had looked forward to these remembrances

97

despite a guilty feeling that he was in some way being disloyal to Mildred.

The feeling of guilt was even stronger as he began to remember now. He remembered nevertheless.

After leaving Carlotta, it was six hard hungry weeks before Jack found work. Every morning he would leave his room in an East End slum, incongruous there in his one good suit, and, having no money for petrol, set off on foot to make the rounds of shops, factories, garages and employment offices. It was the same story as when he had first arrived in London: a hundred men chasing, and sometimes fighting over, every available job.

During the early days of this period he strongly suspected that he was being watched, and once or twice thought he glimpsed Carlotta in passing taxis. His suspicions were confirmed when he got from her a letter, the first of many, protesting her love and pleading that they get together again. He didn't answer the letters; after the first three he began to burn them unopened.

The job he finally cornered was that of chauffeur. An agency sent him to a manor house near Cambridge, where he was interviewed by an Honourable of fifty with blue hair, gaunt face and body and more make-up than she would have needed had she been appearing at the Palladium. Simpering, flirting, she said that really you know references were not all that important, what mattered was if one *took* to a person, there was a word for it but she couldn't think of it, brandy was so bad for the memory.

Jack, having learned during his months with Carlotta that women found him attractive, knew that this was the reason for his acceptance. He waited worriedly for overtures.

Like their mistress, the manor and grounds and the Rolls-

Royce were of advanced years and poor condition. But Jack had a pleasant flat above the gatehouse and ate well with the staff, in addition to drawing a decent wage. With one object in mind he saved his earnings. He wanted to pay a suitable sum to Carlotta and thereby cleanse himself.

As the weeks passed, his role remained strictly that of chauffeur. He relaxed. The letters started arriving from Carlotta. They were burned unread.

He began a friendship with the daughter of the local vicar, a friendship that sneaked into romance over the touched hands of a shared hymn book during the singing of the Twenty-third Psalm. Although at first opposed to the pairing—Jack was, after all, a mere chauffeur—the vicar gradually softened toward his daughter's suitor to the extent of addressing him in a civil tone of voice and allowing him to call at the vicarage on Sunday afternoons. Every possible moment the couple spent together and when apart either telephoned or sent notes of love. Their lovemaking proper never got beyond the kissing and groping stage, which Jack found annoying at the time yet admirable afterwards.

His recent past he considered ugly, a thing of shame. He had been no better than a kept man, a glorified stud. On the other hand, he was grateful to Carlotta for having helped him grow up. He had changed. The harmless amount of cynicism he had acquired and which showed itself in his face—leaner, graver—he thought useful protection in a world for whose toughness he had been ill-prepared by school and the farm.

His romance with the vicar's daughter continued to grow. Her name was Sally. She had brown curly hair, a pert nose and the eyes of a demimondaine; long legs and strident breasts from which the vicar was forever averting his eyes and which Jack was free to explore so long as it was through at least one layer of clothing.

They never argued. There seemed nothing to argue about. They went walking and driving and horse-back riding and to local dances. Since Sally refused to visit the gatehouse flat, their sedentary courting was done mainly in the church, where they simply sat and talked. They would, they decided, "get serious" the following year, when Sally reached twenty-one. In the neighbourhood and at the vicarage it was understood that they had an understanding.

Jack was happy. He didn't know if he was in love, in fact he thought not; but he was happy. He had work, he had a girl, he was regaining his self-respect, he had recovered the health that drink and late nights and an interior existence had impaired. Life was good.

This happiness it was which caused him to be foolishly hospitable the afternoon Carlotta showed up at the flat.

"Hello," he said. "Come in."

Frowning, she stalked past him into the living room. "I've come all the way from Cambridge in a taxi," she said, as if she meant on hands and knees. "Shall I pay him off?"

Jack was cheerfully blunt. "No." He watched her as she circled and sniffed at the room. Her outfit, which formerly he would have admired as sophisticated, he now found ludicrous in its extravagance.

Carlotta turned. "Why haven't you answered my letters?"

"We have nothing to say to each other."

"I could think of a lot to say," she snapped.

"No doubt. But we're through, finished, ended. How about some tea?"

Abruptly, Carlotta changed from a shrew to a figure of tragedy. She began to talk in a tearful voice of the past, their great love, how she knew it was still alive and how they should get back together and let it mature.

Jack stood at the other side of the room shaking his head. He felt nothing; no pity, no hate; nothing. He even had no feelings about her nose-tip, whose bobbing aped and rendered foolish her quasi-poignant speech.

Finally, ridiculously, Carlotta sank to her knees. Jack at once lowered himself into a squat and said, "Yes, do let's sit on the floor. Much more friendly."

Carlotta looked at him aghast. Before she could speak, Jack began to talk about his new life, his job, Sally, his happiness.

Carlotta jumped up in a spittle-flying rage. Happiness, what did he know about it? How could anyone be happy working as a servant and sleeping with the village idiot? He hadn't known what happiness was till she had taught him. She had shown him how to live. She—

At which point Jack got up, strolled to the door and left it open as he went out, calling back, "Don't forget your taxi, darling."

He took off on a walk through the grounds, feeling an immense relief. What he had feared would happen, had, and it had turned out to be not half as searing as expected. Now, he felt sure, he had really seen the last of Carlotta. Soon he would send her some money and the past would be closed.

It was dusk when he returned to the gatehouse. He fumbled his way up the dark stairs, switched on the light, and groaned. He groaned at his own stupidity and at the state of the room. It was a mess. Everything breakable had been broken, everything spillable had been spilled. The curtains had been torn down, piled with other cloths, rugs and all his clothing, then soaked with what looked and smelled to be every liquid the house possessed: water, wine, coal oil, car polish, vinegar, ink and half a can of grey paint. Some paint was also on the walls, formed into words which were usually a part of public lavatory graffiti. In the fireplace lay smouldering ashes; she had burned all his papers.

The kitchen was ankle-deep in smashed crockery, the bathroom mirror had been broken, the bedroom was a snow-drift of shredded sheets. Almost the only thing left untouched in the flat was the telephone. And to this Jack eventually turned for consolation, to hear the voice of reason.

With his back to the vandalism he dialled Sally's number. The vicar answered. His tone was cold and damp like dying hailstones as he said:

"Sally is not here. She has gone away. She does not wish to see you again. Good-bye."

"Wait a minute!" Jack yelled. "What're you talking about?"

"You know very well, sir, what I am talking about."

"I certainly do not."

"Your lady friend. She came to see us. The truth is out."

Jack gritted his teeth. "What truth?"

"Your lady friend is expecting your child."

"What!"

"Poor woman, she only wants you to do the right thing. You are a cad, sir. How lucky that we found out about you in time."

"Listen, where's Sally. I'll come round and explain."

"You will do no such thing. I forbid you to come here. Sally has gone away and does not want to see you again. Good-bye."

The line went dead. Jack let the telephone fall and gave it a kick. He looked around the room in rage and desperation. Tapping his knuckles against his brow he told himself he must have been out of his mind to think that sweet Carlotta would so easily accept rejection.

There was a footstep on the stair. A female step, high heels clicking.

Sally or Carlotta? Jack folded his arms and waited.

In the doorway appeared his employer, the lady of the manor. She had been drinking. Her blue hair was awry and her lipstick smeared. Smilingly she shook a finger at Jack and said, "You're a naughty boy."

"Yes, ma'am."

"I should fire you. But I won't."

"Ma'am?"

"Carlotta phoned up and told me all about you."

"Ah."

"Hiring yourself out as a gigolo and appearing in sex exhibitions. For shame."

Jack sighed.

The Honourable lady swayed into the room. Jack realized she must be even drunker than she seemed for she took no notice of the destruction. She said, still smiling:

"You're a naughty boy but I forgive you. Let's have a little drinkie, shall we, sweet?"

Jack pushed past her and trotted down the stairs. He got in his car and drove off in a rattling protest of gravel.

Here was finished, he thought. He would go north, as far as his money would take him, far enough away from London so that Carlotta would never find him again. Perhaps he could contact Sally and get everything straightened out. But later. For the moment, all he wanted was to get away. Fast.

He roared along the narrow lanes, finding relief for his ripped feelings in speed. He got further relief by cursing

Carlotta in a shout and in terms which made her wall-words seem juvenile.

After an hour he began to think that he might not clear out of the county at all. Why should he let Carlotta win the game? It would be far better to go back, patch things up in the village and then write to tell her that her violence and lies had accomplished nothing. That would be the best possible revenge.

He was driving even faster with the exhilaration of this new idea when he crashed into the wall.

The piercing blast of a car horn brought Jack out of his thoughts. Looking around and in the rear-view mirror he saw that he was driving at a crawl in the centre of the lane and holding up a block of traffic. Putting on speed he moved into the side.

He mused on his accident of thirty years ago. That he had not been killed was something of a miracle. More miraculous was the fact that his injuries had been trivial. The car was a write-off, he merely had lumps on his head and a complementary pain and a pleasant blankness.

But the whole thing, he thought, had been unnecessary. So young, so dramatic, flying off through the night like that. He should have humoured his employer and got her home, cleaned up the flat and gone to see Sally's father. If his word wasn't good enough to lay the lies he could have fetched Carlotta by the scruff of the neck and forced her to tell the truth.

Jack grimaced at the memory of Carlotta, and sighed at the memory of Sally.

The traffic was heavier now: he had reached the downtown area. Soon he turned off at a busy corner to head for his usual car park, when he at last understood why he had been so keen to come down to George Street.

After parking, he walked back, strolled along to Gregory's the gentlemen's outfitters, went in, crossed directly to a counter and said to the salesclerk:

"I'd like to see some of your excellent Scottish ties, please."

5

That same evening the quiet of "West Wind" was broken by a series of reverberating thuds. Tom Brady was coming downstairs.

As it was Saturday night, and as he considered to have done a good week's work, Tom was going out for a beer or two. He had had his third wash of the day, cleaned his teeth with the new toothbrush and combed his hair; and before leaving the room had jotted in his notebook the time of his departure.

Swinging round onto the bottom flight he saw that Mrs Tree was below, in the hall, dusting the hatstand. It occurred to him that nearly every time he came downstairs Mrs Tree was dusting the hatstand. Very tidy woman, Mrs Tree.

He felt himself blushing, which blush was driven away swiftly by alarm as he thought on and at once discarded the notion of asking his landlady if she would care to accompany him for a drink.

"Ah," said Mrs Tree, her face stretching with surprise, "it's you, Mr Brady."

"Good evening, Mrs Tree."

"Going out for a walk?"

"That's right. Been in the house all day."

"I don't get out much myself. I haven't been out shopping in ages."

"Oh yes?"

"Simply ages."

"Well now."

"Which reminds me," said Mrs Tree. "I wanted to ask you about stealing."

Although Tom failed to see the connexion, he was pleased at the chance of putting on a face of officialdom. He asked what exactly did she want to know.

"Well, you must have had lots of experience with thieves and so on."

"Oh, lots, lots."

"They run in types, don't they? I mean, I dare say a man such as yourself could tell a thief just by looking at him, couldn't you?"

"Pretty often, Mrs Tree. Experience y'know."

"Yes. They have long ears or something, don't they?"

Tom, not too sure of his ground, said, "Sometimes. But mostly it's the eyes. Narrow, they are."

He could see she was impressed by the way she blinked widely. "How interesting," she said.

"There's other ways of telling too. But it's technical, highly technical. Be above your head I'm afraid, Mrs Tree."

"I'm sure it would. I know nothing about crime. *Nothing*."

"Naturally."

"And you, Mr Brady, you know so much. You're so clever."

Tom lolled his head in coyness. "Oh well."

"And tell me, by the same token, you'd be able to tell just by looking if a person was not a thief, wouldn't you?"

"Very likely, Mrs Tree."

"I mean, someone who wasn't a *real* thief."

"Oh, absolutely."

"You'd just know, wouldn't you, Mr Brady, you being so experienced? You'd know by the eyes and everything."

"Every time, ma'am, every time."

Mrs Tree nodded briskly. "Thank you, Mr Brady. Most interesting. Well, I won't keep you from your walk. Good evening." Humming, she went into her parlour.

Tom stepped outside. He felt disappointed that the conversation was over. It was nice to enlighten people on the mysteries of police work, especially so with someone like Mrs Tree, who was obviously fascinated and, well, wide-eyed. But there was always the danger of getting trapped by a question he couldn't answer. After all, he didn't know *everything* about police procedure.

With a glance toward the Partridge house—all serene there—Tom set off walking, head high, shoulders back, arms swinging.

He wondered if his disappointment of a minute before was due to the closing not of the topic but of the chat with Mrs Tree. When he felt a blush coming he changed the line of thought and enquired of himself why he had got the idea of asking her to join him for a drink. Romance? Then why be alarmed at the idea? Fear that she would refuse, or disapprove of drinking, or was he afraid of getting involved? It was all the same thing: Romance. Which was ridiculous, an attractive young woman and a man old enough to be her father—nearly.

The blush coming on in full he stopped wondering. Yet to round out the session he did pause to think that he was having some extremely odd thoughts lately.

At the end of the street he crossed to the other side and went into a lane between gardens. It brought him onto a common, open land, an acre of rough ground speckled with the junk of children's games, spiked by the occasional tree

109

and surrounded by the backs of houses. He followed the path which short-cutted to the nearest shopping district, Dimple Hill's business section.

Partway across the common Tom got the feeling that there was someone behind; more, that he was being followed. He stopped and slowly turned. Being twilight, visibility was none too perfect. But had he not glimpsed a movement by that far eucalyptus tree? Certainly there was nothing now, but before, at the moment of turning, he was sure he had seen what could have been a figure stepping sharply behind the tree and out of view.

After watching for a minute, eyes straining through the gloom, Tom decided he must have been mistaken. And even if there was someone behind the tree, why should he be concerned? He was the follower, not the followed.

Walking on, he crossed the common and went down another lane between gardens, came out onto a main road and turned toward the cluster of commercial lights.

A passing car screeched its brakes in avoiding a boy who unexpectedly swerved his bicycle. The driver stretched his neck in his collar to deliver a stream of pungent abuse, the boy made an obscene sign with his fingers.

Tom shook his head at the fleeting incident and thought of what, in his days as a policeman, he would have had to say to the boy. He would have had him trembling in no time flat.

Next he was reminded pleasurably of the time he had appeared in court as the witness to an accident on George Street. He had impressed everyone, he knew, by the professional way he had given evidence (in fact he had been surprised that the magistrate made no comment on this). It had been a day full of interest, and what was more they had paid his expenses. The whole thing had started like the incident just now. He had heard a squeal of brakes followed by a great crash and had turned to see . . .

Tom's reminiscence faltered. His pleasure went. He frowned. In a moment he admitted to himself that yes, he had not actually seen the accident, although he had said he had. Really, all he had done was hear it happen. Glancing around guiltily Tom further admitted that no, it had not been quite the right thing to do, saying he had been a witness, plus swearing to this in the box. Well, all right then, it had been wrong. Very wrong. Perhaps criminal. And hadn't he exaggerated his expenses the teeniest bit?

His posture sagged, his hands met one another behind. For the first time in days he lost his cheeriness. He couldn't imagine what had got into him to think this way.

But since thinking this way he was, he asked himself what could be so clever about a grown man making a young boy tremble.

He slooped along to a pub and went in.

It was a large room with a centre bar, a room bare and cold. The walls and floor were tiled. There were no chairs or stools. There were no pictures, no music, no bar-room games, no women—nothing in fact to distract the attention from the serious Australian business of drinking.

Early yet, there were no more than a dozen men lounged around the bar. Leaning there too, Tom, in order to assuage his hurt feelings, asked for a whisky. He drank it and ordered another.

As the door opened he turned his head in an idle movement and saw Jack Partridge.

Jack paused on the threshold. His eyes had met Tom Brady's and moved away. Now he didn't know what he should do, didn't know why in the first place he had started

111

to follow the other after seeing him in the distance. Jack had left the house merely to get away from Mildred's amused questions on why he had bought four plaid ties, an Irish linen handkerchief, two pairs of German socks and a wallet made in Czechoslovakia.

He thought that it would be silly to back out again. Moving to the bar, two yards and two men from where Tom Brady stood, he ordered a gin, his choice of a short drink stemming from the fact that he wanted to get it down quickly and leave.

He glanced along the bar, saw there was now only one man between Brady and himself, lifted his glass and drained it at a swallow.

Tom was uncomfortable. He had variable feelings about Jack Partridge. Just as a bed can stimulate, depress or calm, reminding of sex, sickness or sleep, depending on the momentary state of the viewer's mind, so Tom's attitude toward Partridge changed from hour to hour and scene to scene. When sullen from recent sleep he thought of him with dislike, when mellow in tiredness with something like gratitude; before meals he saw him grumpily, afterwards with tolerance. Partridge peering through his picture window was sly, driving grandly past in his car sinister, at work a fugitive from justice made doubly villainous by being financially big, strolling with his wife around the lawn simply another bloke, playing with his grandchildren a fine and lucky man, pausing to look at a sunset a likeable person. What was he when leaning on a bar having a drink?

Tom drained his whisky and ordered another.

Now what's this? thought Jack. I drink mine straight down, he drinks his straight down. Is it going to be follow-the-leader again?

Deciding against leaving at once, Jack ordered a second gin. He could already feel the first one at work, embracing the two beers he had drunk at home. Indeed, as the embracing went on it began to turn into an affair of some passion, the heat from which rose smilingly to Jack's head.

Served, he moved a step closer along the bar toward Tom Brady, who, he saw, was also being given another drink.

Using the man between as a shield, peering around in front of his shoulder, Jack had his first close, careful look at the new resident of Gormon Lane. Though the scrutiny told him little, being able to make it gave him deep satisfaction. In any case, there was nothing the least bit terrifying about Brady. The reverse; his frayed cuff, the shaving nick on his cheek, the bag in his trousers, these made him human and fallible.

Tom drank his whisky, not fast yet still at the one intake, put down his glass and looked along the bar to counter the stare he had been feeling for the past two minutes. Partridge turned away and lifted his drink.

Tom took a step sideways toward the man between to get a good close look at the next man along. Partridge, he saw with surprise, seemed to have aged in the short time since the meeting on George Street. He was more lined, less solid-looking, darker around the eyes. Or perhaps the meeting had been too brief for anything other than recognition. Or again, perhaps it was just that the poor fella was not feeling well.

While gazing at a row of beer bottles, which, curiously, appeared to be leaning out of the upright, Jack was wondering for the first time how he felt about the man who had so suddenly and radically changed his life. Did he hate Tom Brady? Not really. In fact not at all. Dislike him? No. Fear him? Not any more. Like him then? Of course not. Well what? Well nothing. And anyway, who cared?

Jack saw that his gin was gone and ordered another.

It occurred to Tom, with shock and embarrassment, that Jack Partridge's seedy look might be caused not by something physical, that what weighed him down was the constant surveillance and the fact that he was well aware of its reason. Tom had not thought of this before, of what his actions might be doing to the other's emotions and nerves. No wonder he was looking like death, poor bloke.

Tom gave a melancholy belch and ordered another drink.

Served at the same time, Jack Partridge and Tom Brady lifted their glasses and turned toward one another. The man between had gone; they were separated by only a yard of space. They stared in silence, for the moment lost.

Jack recovered first. From the superior calm brought by his acceptance of the inevitable, he nodded his glass and said, "Cheers."

"Er, cheers," said Tom.

Not taking their eyes from each other, they drank, slowly emptying the glasses. Tom asked, "Have one on me?"

"Thank you."

As Tom turned to order he noticed that his vision blurred, like watching a film that was sweeping a scene too fast. He shook his head and asked the barman for two more of the same.

Because of a certain quavering in his legs, Jack hitched most of his upper body onto the bar. He told himself he was in a tricky situation. He would have to watch what he said. But he didn't really care.

Tom asked, "Did you follow me across the common to-night?"

"Yes," said Jack, and frowned for not having replied in the negative. "Yes, I certainly did."

"Why?"

"No idea. To see where you were going, I suppose."

"I was going here."

"Oh."

They were served with their drinks, which they delicately drained. Jack said, "My shout now, okay?"

"Okay."

After ordering, Jack said, "I'm an Australian."

"You could be at that," Tom admitted.

Jack smiled craftily to himself. Tom Brady did not know the whole story. I am a smart one, thought Jack. I am also a getting drunk one. He said, "You're not so brainy, mate. I'm not Australian at all."

"Makes no difference."

Jack was crestfallen. "I don't suppose it does really."

"Could be Chi-bloody-nese and it still wouldn't make no difference."

The new drinks arrived. "Two more," said Jack, and swallowed his gin in a gulp. Setting down the glass he tried to get his thoughts in order. He was, he realized, quite drunk, although five minutes ago he had been sober. The things he had been saying were foolish. He should be asking, anyway, not telling.

"Still with the police, eh?"

"No."

"You're not?"

"No."

"But they're in on this, aren't they?"

"No," said Tom: then thought how stupid he was being.

115

He should not give it away that he alone knew of Partridge's involvement in the murder. Partridge might do something funny. He *had* followed across the common.

Jack asked, "Surely someone else knows about me?"

"Not a soul," said Tom proudly. "It's all mine."

Again Jack tried to marshal his thoughts. Something was wrong somewhere. He asked, "What about your family? Told them?"

"Got no family," said Tom, feeling a gruffness in his throat. He cleared it away and told himself to stop acting as if he was drunk. He was not in the least bit drunk. He had only had . . . Yes, he was drunk. But still thinking clearly and coolly and cleverly.

"Listen," he said. "It's my turn to ask a question. You've been asking *all* the questions."

"Sorry."

"It's not fair."

"Well, sorry."

"Right. Now then." Tom frowned and pressed his brow, trying to bring a question to mind. "Er . . . ?"

"How about my name?"

"That's it! Capstan wasn't your real name, eh?"

"No. We picked it off a cigarette box. Armstrong's my real name."

"Well there you are," said Tom, not sure of what he meant.

The drinks came. The two men toasted one another and emptied their glasses. Tom asked for a repeat.

Jack said, "You're not a private detective?"

"Nope."

"Don't work at anything?"

"Retired."

"Boring I should imagine."

116

"I'll say." Tom gave up the effort of trying to think straight. He let his mind and muscles slump. "The old days was best."

Jack's mental effort had already been given up. "The good old days," he said.

"Nothing's the same any more, is it?"

"Nothing."

"Even food hasn't the same flavour."

"London in the spring," murmured Jack, suddenly overcome with sentiment. His eyes turned watery.

Both men stared into space, until they noticed that the drinks had been served. Tom reached for the glasses—and knocked them over. He ordered refills, telling the barman to be more careful next time.

He turned to Jack. "You're lucky, you are. Family and everything."

"Yes."

"And you were lucky in the old days too."

Jack recovered from his emotion. "I suppose so."

"Got clean away."

"It wasn't easy."

"It wasn't easy for me either."

"No?"

The drinks were served, were drained, were ordered to be repeated. The room was filling and the noise growing, both factors causing Tom and Jack to draw closer together.

It was Tom's eyes now that filled with tears. "Hard on me it was," he said. "You shouldn't a done it."

"Sorry, old man."

"Leaving me in the lurch like that."

"Sorry."

"Never did get me promotion."

"No?"

117

Tom shook his head heavily. A single tear trickled down his cheek. "Passed over. Passed over like an old glove."

Jack put an arm around Tom's shoulder and tutted in sympathy. Tom said a hoarse, "Lost all me ambition after that."

"I couldn't help it, Mr Brady."

"Tom. You can call me Tom."

"And you may call me Jack."

They shook hands, solemnly, sadly, delightedly.

"No, I couldn't help it, Tom."

"Oh well."

The fresh drinks appeared. Jack, after spilling half his gin on his hand, managed to get the other half in his mouth. All Tom's whisky ran down his chin and into his collar.

"Two more, please," called Jack. He removed his arm from the other's shoulder the better to support himself on the bar. "If I could've helped it," he said, "I would've helped it."

"I'm sure you would, Jack."

"I'm the helpful sort. You know?"

"Yes," said Tom, with a snap bringing up his head, which had been sinking. "I know what you mean, Sam."

"Jack."

"Tom's the name."

"Help anyone, I would. Help an old blind dog I would." Again Jack felt emotion rising as he saw himself helping an old blind dog.

The drinks came. Tom took his glass in both hands, raised it, tilted back his head and with great care poured the whisky into his nostrils. He snorted like a surfacing swimmer.

Jack gave his drink a look of distaste and pushed it aside. He said, "You just don't realize what a kind person I am."

"Yes I do," said Tom, wiping his face with his tie. "As kind as could be."

"No you don't," sniffed Jack.

"Yes I do. Accidents will happen."

"Mildred appreciates me."

"I didn't really see it y'know. I only heard the crash. Don't tell no one."

"A good sort is Mildred."

"Was she really your lawful wedded wife, Stan?"

"I've got to go," slurred Jack. His face was the colour of a winter's dawn. So much of his body was being supported by the bar that only his toes were touching the floor. "What say?"

"I said let's have another."

Jack made no answer. He stared dopily down.

Raising his once-more sinking head Tom bellowed "Service!" at the white jacket in front of him. "Gin, whisky," he added. His head sank. He lifted it again to ask, "What?"

The barman repeated in a loud firm voice that he thought they had both had enough. He was cutting them off.

Tom pushed himself up to arms' length, glared with reasonable accuracy at the mist of pink face and snarled, "Whisky and gin. Quick. Or I'll bash your face in."

I'll bash your face in.

The words cut their way viciously into Jack Partridge's stupified brain. He thought of a face being bashed in, pictured the blood, heard a scream. Abruptly and forcefully he shoved himself away from the bar: so forcefully that only the density of the crowd prevented him from falling backwards. Shock brought him several degrees less drunk.

He had to get out. He had to get away. What had he

119

been saying? How long had he been here talking to this man?

Swinging round he lurched through the crowd, reached the door and got himself outside. He began to stagger along as fast as he could go, one hand repeatedly stabbing at the wall for support. Faster he went when a familiar voice yelled from behind:

"Wait for me!"

He had to get away before he said anything else, if he had not said too much already. He had to get home to Mildred.

Although he seemed to be thinking clearly, his body might have belonged to another man. It was either misinterpreting or downright ignoring his brain's orders. No matter how hard he concentrated, frowning, glaring, he was unable to keep a straight course.

He tacked across the pavement, lurching in and out of the gutter and bumping against the wall. Once it was not a wall but a shop window he bumped against and the resulting boom sent him reeling with fright halfway across the road.

He weaved past a group of teenagers, who laughed at him and shouted names, reached the lane which led to the common and stopped to look back. Tom Brady was coming along at an erratic yet implacable pace. He waved and shouted.

Jack blundered into the lane. Darkness made him hit the fence, veer off and hit the fence opposite and from there sprawl out on his belly. Behind him he could hear Tom Brady's voice raised in song.

He scrambled up and shot forward, running in a crouch, at times on all fours as his fingertips flapped the ground ahead. Reaching the lane end he made a sharp turn, got sufficiently far from the path to be unseen and let himself fall flat.

Tom Brady came onto the common singing. He tripped and went into a stagger, recovered, leaned on a tree for a moment, laughed heartily and went on his way.

Jack thought he would lie still for a few minutes, let Brady get well in front. The rest would give his body time to catch up with the sobriety of his head.

He lay still and fell asleep.

Tom stopped at the gate of "West Wind." His eyes were glazed, the muscles of his face slack. He felt one second like sleeping, the next like laughing. His knees began to give way; he put his arms around the gatepost.

He looked up the street, swivelled his head with difficulty and looked down the street. Had he lost something? Or someone? He was sure that not long ago he had not been alone.

This question he forgot on noticing how the lights from the windows and the street lamps seemed to be jumping, swerving, fusing and scattering. It was better than a cartoon. He laughed.

When his laugh spluttered off his attention was next wobblingly arrested by the street itself. It was so quiet, so lonely. Poor old street. Thinking he would cheer it up with a song he lifted his head and boomed:

> *She was poor but she was honest,*
> *Victim of the Squire's whim,*
> *First he loved her, then he left her,*
> *And she lost her honest name.*

Farther along, a head poked itself out of a doorway. The curtains in two lighted windows of Mrs Tree's house moved aside to show cautious silhouettes.

> See the little old-world village
> Where her aged parents live,
> Drinking the champagne she sends them,
> But they never can forgive.

The front door of "West Wind" opened. A small figure came out, threw all around a worried glance, trotted in a huddle to the gate, looked up and asked, "Is that you, Mr Brady?"

> Standing on the bridge at midnight,
> She says: 'Farewell, blighted love.'
> There's a scream, a splash—Good Heavens!
> What is she a-doing of?

"Mr Brady, please."

Tom recognized his landlady. He said, "Evening, old girl. Nothing like a song or two, is there?"

"I think it's time you came in, Mr Brady."

"I'll just give you another one."

"Not now. You've sung enough for the present."

"Yes, fair do's. It's your turn. Quiet everybody!"

"Now now, Mr Brady."

"Give us that one about Maggie with the bloomers red, which never to themselves had said, come in, lads, come in."

"Now now. You'll wake the neighbours."

Tom leaned around the gatepost. "Old girl, did anyone ever tell you that you've got very pretty eyes?"

Mrs Tree coughed. "Please come inside, Mr Brady."

Tom pouted. "No."

"I'll, er, I'll give you a drink."

"That's right, let's all have a drink. Service!"

"Shhh," said Mrs Tree, opening the gate. "Do come in."

Tom released the gatepost. Immediately he weaved backwards, overbalanced and sat down with a thud. He mumbled, "Bash his face in." He was about to lower himself fully onto the nice friendly neighbourhood pavement when his arm was grabbed and tugged.

"Up, up."

Grumbling, he got up, flung an arm around Mrs Tree's shoulder and stumbled along beside her into the house. Going to the foot of the stairs he again raised his voice in song:

> It's the same the whole world over,
> It's the poor what gets the blame,
> It's the rich what gets the gravy,
> Ain't it all a bleeding shame.

"Sssshhhh!" hissed Mrs Tree. "Come on, up we go."

"No."

"Yes yes, time for beddy-byes."

"I'm not moving," said Tom, "until you give me a kiss."

"Mr Brady!"

He grinned down into her face. "Just one little kiss."

"And then you'll go upstairs?"

"I will."

"Promise?"

"Scout's honour."

Their lips met in a great smack. Tom laughed and began to climb, still holding tightly to Mrs Tree, who gasped out words of encouragement between telling him that he really was a rather naughty boy.

At the top of the first flight they halted to change positions, during which tricky maneuver Tom managed to poke his elbow neatly into Mrs Tree's ear. Ready for off, they were held back by a bedroom door opening.

Tom saw in the doorway a figure and heard it gasp. Another gasp came from Mrs Tree. The door closed and Tom found himself being urged upward with tugs and hisses. He blundered up, got into his room and collapsed in the armchair.

"Poor but honest," he said, "that's me. Where's the drink?"

"Coming right away. Don't move, don't sing."

"No songs?"

"No."

"Well, I'll go to sleep then."

"No no, I want to *talk* to you."

Mrs Tree left the room. Tom bent forward to untie his shoelaces. The task loomed as an absolute impossibility. He leaned back and closed his eyes. When he opened them again Mrs Tree was coming in with a tumbler full of red liquid.

"Wine," she said.

Tom took the glass, emptied it in three gulps and set it on the table. He looked straight ahead. The room was swaying. Or perhaps it was himself. He sagged down and let his head sink. He could hear Mrs Tree talking, and, though he couldn't make out the words, he had the feeling that she was saying something important.

"Huh?" he said. "What was that?"

"Your investigation, Mr Brady."

"Ah yes." He smiled cunningly.

"It's going well?"

"Ho ho."

"I see."

"Cornered. He's trapped."

"Who?"

"The guilty party."

"Mr Brady, I—"

124

"You can call me Tom."

"Thank you. You said—"

"Listen." Tom lifted his head, tried to focus, failed and asked, "Did anyone ever tell you . . ." He was unable to finish. His head fell back.

"Tom, who is the guilty party?"

"'S a secret."

"You said *he*. It's a man?"

"Course."

"And you are investigating only one person?"

"Course."

"It couldn't be me then."

Tom gave his head a negative roll. He didn't understand what anyone was saying, not even himself. He wanted to go to sleep. He said as much into the flow of Mrs Tree's talk.

"But, Tom, you must tell me about the guilty party."

Tom sat up. "Ambition."

Mrs Tree asked, "What's the guilty party done?"

Tom heard and understood the question. He digested it with care. He nodded. His face became severe. Raising a limp forefinger on a weaving hand he told the wall:

"In this street there lives a murderer."

"Oh dear," said Mrs Tree.

Tom liked his statement. It was well rounded, you might say poetic. He made it again. Smiling, he repeated it to himself. He was about to slump down when Mrs Tree spoke.

"So all this time," she said, "you have been investigating someone who's done a murder?"

"I have. In this street."

"What's his name, Tom?"

"'S a secret."

"You can give me a hint though, mm?"

"No."

"Oh, come on, you can give Janet a hint."

Whoever Janet might be, Tom was not going to give her anything. He had to get some sleep. Sleep. The very echo of the word was overpowering. His head and shoulders began to sink toward his knees.

"Oh, you are naughty," said Mrs Tree. "Tell me what he looks like, at least. Describe him."

Describe him. The order, repeated often, was well remembered. Constable Thomas Brady lifted his head, pushed mightily to get himself to his feet, stood at swaying attention with hands flat against his hips and ground out in a monotone:

"Suspect is six feet tall, weighs in the vicinity of fourteen stone, has fresh complexion, blue or grey eyes, brown hair, was last seen wearing a pin-stripe suit."

Tom saluted, stepped forward, fell onto the bed and passed out.

6

Sunday morning. Gormon Lane lay in a stupor of laziness. The springtime sun shone on a man leaning thoughtfully against a lawnmower, on Mildred Partridge as she sat in a deck chair waiting for her husband to wake up, and through a bay window on a small yellow bird that watched warily the endless pacing of its mistress.

Like a boxer after a quick victory, Janet could not keep still. So torn was she by varying emotions—relief, embarrassment, pleasure, dismay, shuddery excitement—that she was unable to settle herself to savouring or suffering any particular one.

The making of breakfast had been a catastrophe of three broken plates, overfried bacon and dropped cutlery; and she had come close to upsetting Mr East's tray at the foot of the stairs. Now that everyone was served, she found it impossible to face thoughts of her own breakfast. All she could manage was tea, cup after cup.

What a night! she exclaimed to herself for the fiftieth time. A night of discovery and shock and, you could almost say, passion.

Janet continued to wander around the parlour, sitting briefly, straightening an ornament which she had un-

127

straightened on the previous circuit, glancing out of the window and swooping on her canary an endearment from which the bird retreated to flatten itself against the farther bars. What a night!

First Mr Brady—Tom, that is, he had been most insistent that she use his first name, that they put their relationship on a more intimate level—first Tom singing outside after having dined rather well, a song which seemed somewhat risqué at that, then herself going out to coax him in. How could she have ever brought herself to do anything so brave and outrageous? Well, for one her nerves were at rest from the outing earlier in the day, for another the person involved was Tom. He was such a man. So firm. The way he had stolen a kiss, the first kiss in more than twenty years, she could not have refused had she wanted. And she hadn't wanted (blushing, forgetting the unpleasant whisky-flavoured sloppiness), not really. In either case, he was too strong to resist. Strong and firm and very naughty. But sweet to say she had pretty eyes.

Janet stopped in front of the mirror. She blinked, rolled her eyes and stretched them wide, winked first one and then the other, turned to the side and glared at her reflection dramatically.

"Yes," she said, swinging round and opening her arms toward the sunlight, "I have pretty eyes." At which moment, filled as they were with delight, pretty her eyes undoubtedly were.

She began walking again, and her smile faded: in her reliving of the previous night she had reached the point where Mr East had opened his door, drawn of course by the noise, and had seen her in the arms of Tom Brady. Janet cringed with mortification, remembering the expression on her boarder's face and his gasp of outrage and the way his hands had tumbled over one another in their haste to get the door closed. It had been a horrible half minute.

Now Janet's face lightened once more as her thoughts hurried gratefully away, on to the evening's most satisfying aspect, her discovery, through clever questioning, that her fears were unfounded. She was not being investigated after all. Tom's appearance on that particular day had been coincidental. She should have seen it for herself, in his attitude, in their rapport, in his bewilderment at some of her pointed remarks, which she had taken for evasion. She was free.

Janet ventured a snatch of song. She felt young, vigorous and, yes, beautiful. She felt wanted. She also felt like another cup of tea.

Waltzing into the kitchen she put on the whistling kettle, stoked the teapot and set out crockery. Going back into her parlour until the kettle boiled, circling, she reached the window, when again she recalled the final revelation of the night before. Filled with a goose-fleshy thrill she looked out of the window and thought, In this street there lives a murderer. Fantastic. But certainly true. Tom had said so. It was his reason for living here. He was doing special undercover work. Highly dangerous. Top Secret. He had told her about it because of their, well, rapport. No one else knew, surely.

Janet clutched her waist and shivered. She was thrilled and excited and flattered to the skies. Free, beautiful, desired *and* informed. It was nearly too much.

The kettle whistled.

Janet hurried into the kitchen to make her tea. What a night, she thought again. There hadn't been such a night at "West Wind" for years, not since the time the chimney set on fire and the fire brigade came. Tom Brady had brought some light into the house. Marvellous.

She carried her cup into the parlour and made herself

sit. Even so, as she drank her feet kept up a rapid tapping.

There was a knock on the door. Gaily, Janet called, "Come in."

Into the room stepped Mr East. Before Janet could start to blush she saw the suitcase in his hand. She said, "Oh?"

Mr East put down the case, smoothed himself. His narrow face was pale with severity, heightening the blackness and glitter of his close-set eyes.

"Mrs Tree," he announced, "I am leaving."

"Er, really, Mr East?"

"Really, Mrs Tree. I don't think I need state my reasons."

Janet put down her cup and rose, head erect. "But it so happens that I think you do, Mr East."

"Come now"—a narrow smile curving under the parrot nose—"that would be hardly necessary."

"I disagree. And there's the question of notice."

"Under the circumstances, madame, I believe I am within my rights in not giving the customary notice. And luckily, this is Sunday. My rent is all paid up. I shall not have to ask for a rebate."

"Rebate indeed!"

"I merely stopped in to notify you of my departure, to tell you that someone will be calling for my trunk in due course, and to express my disappointment."

"Now just—"

"No, you cannot prevail upon me to stay. My mind is made up."

"Good. I'm glad you're going."

Mr East blanched. "Well!"

"And what exactly do you mean by 'disappointment'?"

Mr East wriggled his ruffled self. "I am disappointed that this residence is no longer respectable. As if the snoring and

130

stamping were not bad enough, now we have drinking, singing, raucous laughter and—since you force me to say it I will—and *cuddling*."

Janet burst into a redness of embarrassment and anger. "Mr East!"

He smirked.

"That's libel!"

"Slander," said the undertaker's assistant. "No, I mean it's neither. The truth is the truth."

"You misconstrued the situation."

"I know what I saw, Mrs Tree. And I know what I heard."

"Heard?"

"Remember, my room is directly beneath that of our mutual friend. I use the term loosely, of course. Mr Brady could never be a friend of mine. He's not, well, not quite of my milieu."

"Mr Brady is a fine man," said Janet weakly, feeling dislocated, unable to keep up with the stream of insult and innuendo.

Another smirk. "To be sure, to be sure."

"No one could wish for a better lodger."

Mr East winced. "Your language . . ."

"At least he's a man, not a mouldy vegetable."

"Deplorable taste, madame."

"Get," said Janet, mustering all her majesty, "out."

Mr East bent at the knees, jerked up his case, said, "Deplorable," and left the room without closing the door— which allowed Janet the satisfaction of doing so slammingly. But a second later Mr East had the last slam with the door of the house.

Janet stamped her feet and wept with rage and frustration.

131

Mildred Partridge was reading a book she found she could put down with the greatest of ease; so she put it down. Leaning back her head against the canvas of the deck chair, closing her eyes against the brightness of the sun, she went back to the question of why Jack had been so late last night.

He had said he was going out for a walk; she had expected him at about nine. He still had not come home by eleven. At eleven-thirty, yawning, eyes adroop, she had gone to bed, and was alone when she fell asleep.

Where could he have been? What could he have been doing? He was sleeping so soundly that it might have been dawn when he came back. He wasn't one for poker games, it wasn't a case of the car breaking down somewhere because he was on foot, he belonged to none of those men's clubs where they went in for orgies that were supposed to be business meetings, he wasn't a drinking man and he could never be dragged to a night club.

Ticking off on her fingers the aberrations of the male sex, Mildred found that she had only one left: womanizing.

She laughed briefly at the fantasy of this angle in relation to her Jack before starting to examine it with care.

He was the right age, the dangerous age when men felt it was now or never. He still had his looks. He *had* been different lately, looking tired, going off on his own for walks or drives and always saying when asked where he'd been, "Oh, nowhere in particular, just here and there." And what about his change in attitude?—wanting to help around the house, one day bringing her a bunch of flowers, once taking her out to dinner. Was this not the sign of a guilty conscience?

132

Mildred realized with alarm that she was building a strong case for the prosecution. Then she remembered what had happened after their dinner out and knew she was being foolish.

Bathed with relief and love she got up, went into the house and through to the master bedroom. She wanted to do something for Jack to atone for her suspicions, some menial service.

He was soundly asleep. She hadn't the heart to wake him up. After gazing fondly at his crumpled face for a while she returned to the deck chair and picked up her book.

And remembered those odd things he had brought home yesterday afternoon and had seemed reluctant to let her see. He couldn't explain why he had bought them. It had been funny then. It wasn't funny now because now there was an explanation. They were presents for his woman.

Reason asked: did women use men's socks, handkerchiefs, ties and wallets?

Mildred laughed at herself for her foolishness. She opened the book and wondered if the woman lived in Dimple Hill.

Janet's weeping had not lasted long. She had discovered greater release in stalking around the room while vilifying Mr East in a low, harsh voice. The most telling point she made was to ordain him Gormon Lane's resident murderer. She gloated over this like a bitch over her best friend's unwanted conception. Mr East was so perfect as the slimy, sinister, feelingless killer. Unfortunately, too much so to be true. And for another thing, he didn't fit the description.

Janet's disappointment was eased by her growing curios-

133

ity about whom Tom had meant. She no longer thought on the revelation of last night with chilly excitement but with great interest . . . and something else about which she was unsure.

Scolding herself for not having questioned Tom more closely, she stood in the window bay and looked out. Had any wives died lately? No, not for years. Had anyone come into money? Not as far as she knew. Well, who fitted the description?

She looked at all the houses in view and thought of those out of sight, picturing the male occupants. Many fitted. Except in the age department, for try as she might she was unable to recall how old Tom had said the man was, and she had never given much thought to age anyway. In fact, so thrilled had she been to hear the murderer described that she had listened with only half an ear. Some details, however, she had firmly retained. Tall and of solid build, fresh complexion, brown hair. Yes, many men in the street fitted. She began to go through their names.

At a tap on the door she called, "Come in, Mr Snow," knowing the author of the tap by its dry hesitancy, the same as the cough he used to prompt himself into speech.

Mr Snow came in. Behind him in the hall stood two suitcases. Janet said, "What?"

A delicate young man with a red face and red hair, the divinity student repeated his tap vocally and said a worried, "Good morning, Mrs Tree."

Forgetting manners in her astonishment, Janet squeaked, "You're not leaving too?"

Mr Snow regretted, he couldn't express how much he regretted, that leaving he was. Not that it had been an easy decision. He had been wrestling with his conscience all morning, ever since Mr East had informed of the sights, which matched with the sounds, of the night before. He had his position to consider.

Mr Snow was so manifestly distressed that Janet could feel no anger, despite what he implied. She felt only a sense of loss.

"You can't believe everything you hear," she feebly offered."

"No, Mrs Tree. But unfortunately, everything fits together."

"I don't follow."

"I mean, you've had Mr Brady to tea, haven't you?"

"Well, yes."

Mr Snow swallowed. "We were never asked to tea, were we?"

"Well, no."

"And once"—he seemed to be fighting against tears—"once I even saw his boots outside his door. You had *polished* them."

Janet averted her eyes. "I'm terribly sorry."

"I shall pray for you, Mrs Tree," he murmured. "Goodbye." Retreating softly he closed the door.

Janet let herself flop into a chair. She had no time to regret the passing of Mr Snow as a person of long-term acquaintance, for she was suddenly struck by the enormity of her situation. She had lost two boarders. Her income had been brutally reduced by two thirds. Now she was in serious straits.

Janet gazed around in bewilderment. In less than an hour her world had changed from being rosy and secure to being rickety and grey. It couldn't be true. She must be dreaming. It was too too tragic.

Janet shook her head sternly and told herself to accept the truth, stop leaning toward self-pity and do some posi-

135

tive thinking. She still had her pension and Tom Brady was in residence, but she must needs rent the two vacated rooms at once. This might not be easy. Dimple Hill was so residential. The main commercial areas were miles away. The local business section was staffed by local people. Come to think of it, the vicinity had no other guest houses. They were not needed.

The more Janet thought about filling her two rooms, the more impossible it seemed. She saw months going by and money being spent on advertizing. Though she would not of course starve, there would be nothing for extras and there would be no more Outings. Unless she went back to her acquiring expeditions. Which, in spite of there being no investigation, so far as she knew, would still be highly dangerous in the Sydney area. The only answer was making trips, as per the former decision. And that held no appeal.

Janet got up and began to circle the room. Inexplicably, she found herself unable to keep on the problem of her financial future. Her mind persisted in reverting to the fact that in Gormon Lane there lived a murderer. Or perhaps it was not inexplicable. Were the two connected?

"Do you know what time it is?"

The voice came cruelly into Jack Partridge's sleep, snatching him to the alien surface of consciousness, like a fish hooked fast from the deep. He opened one eye, saw the familiar wall of his bedroom, recognized the voice as belonging to his wife. The eye was burning. As he closed it he became aware of the pounding pain in his temples. Smothering a moan he feigned sleep.

Mildred looked at Jack's clothes lying on and around a

chair. She recalled the scene of agonizing discovery from a thousand eternal-triangle novels. Stepping to the chair she lifted her husband's jacket. Fearfully, she examined at close range the shoulders and lapels. She was relieved to find nothing there, no long silky hairs. She looked at his shirt collar, his handkerchief. No lipstick. Even so, she mused, men were clever about such things.

Querulously she said, "Jack? Are you awake? Do you know it's nearly eleven?"

"Mmmm," he mumbled, as if slowly waking up, giving himself time to think. It was coming back now, the night before. He remembered sleeping on the common, staggering home at two in the morning to find his wife asleep and creeping quietly into bed beside her.

"Jack?"

"Yes," he said, keeping his burning eyes closed. "I'm awake."

"What happened last night?"

"How d'you mean?"

"Where *were* you?"

Jack thought he had better stick close to the truth as far as his drinking was concerned. He couldn't go through the torture of pretending not to be hungover. He said:

"Met a mate of mine. A car dealer. I sold him a truck, sight unseen, and we had a few drinks to seal the deal. I got fairly tight."

"What time was it when you got home?"

"Late. Almost midnight, I should think. I really don't remember."

Mildred was mollified enough to be able to turn derisive. "A nice thing. Getting sloshed at your age."

Jack reflected in passing that a fortnight ago Mildred would not have dreamt of questioning his right to get drunk if he wanted. He said, "Anyway, if it's any consolation to you, I feel lousy."

"So you should."

Jack thought she was going too far. He opened his eyes and looked round frowning. "All right, woman," he growled. "That's enough. Cut the gab and leave me alone. I want to sleep."

Mildred smiled with relief and love. Her suspicions were dead. This was her own masterful Jack of old who loved her and she had been thinking like a fool.

"Go on," said Jack. "Hop it."

"Yes, dear," said Mildred meekly, happily, and hurried off to bake her husband his favourite dish, apple pie.

Jack sank his head back into the pillow, closed his eyes and gave himself up to the luxury of a groan.

After a while his mind went to the time before his sleep on the common, to the scene in the pub. What, he asked himself with anguish, had he said? How far had his drunkenness allowed him to go? The scene was hazy, except for the first part, when he had admitted that he was the one connected with the London murder and even told about the name Capstan. What worse could he have done than that?

Jack groaned again.

But what seemed more to the point, he thought, was what Tom Brady had given away. He was no longer a policeman. He was not a private detective. He had not told the police, or anyone else. Why had he kept it to himself? What was his game? Or perhaps his game was over now, now that he had a definite admission. Perhaps at this moment he was making a statement to the police.

Jack found that thinking made his headache worse. He contented himself with suffering his hangover.

Janet paused in drinking her ninth cup of tea of the morning. She paused to smile. For half an hour, ever since realizing what was the connexion between her need of money and the murderer, she had been trying to think of a word. Now the word had finally come. It was *blackmail*.

Tom Brady awoke. He rolled over onto his back, when he saw that he was lying on top of the covers, athwart the bed, and that he had all his clothes on. He sat up. His head felt muzzy, as though he were slightly drunk. From the angle of the sun chinking between the curtains he figured the time and knew he had slept through most of his hangover.

He got off the bed, stripped and put on his shabby fawn robe with the braid edging. Opening the door he felt a momentary nausea at the tray of cold, grease-white breakfast. He took a deep breath, stepped over the tray and set off in a creep for the bathroom to bring his brain alive.

When he returned, steaming from a hot bath, he put on clean linen and added the rest of his clothes. He lowered himself gently into the armchair to put on his boots.

His stomach felt fine, he was not shaking and the faint throb in his head, which burst into strength only with sudden movement and which he knew would soon fade, was there solely because of the wine. He supposed he must have drunk the wine. He certainly remembered being given a glass. And that was the last thing he did remember. The rest . . .

He clenched his hands in embarrassment. Kissing Mrs

Tree and everything. What did she think of it all? What was he going to say to her when they met?

With ten fingers to his brow he forced himself to recall every detail, starting from his chorus outside the house. He sighed heavily. What *would* he say to Mrs Tree when next they met?

He laced his boots and got up. In spite of dreading a meeting, he was going to take a chance on bringing one about. The three glasses of water he had drunk in the bathroom had helped, but to complete the cure he needed as many cups of coffee followed by some solid food.

He left the room, went with the tenderness his head and the situation warranted down the first flight of stairs and with greater tenderness down the second. He held his breath until he had got past the door of Mrs Tree's parlour; he closed his eyes to encourage silence until he had got the front door open.

Backing out he drew the door closed gently, took six delicate steps in reverse and turned. And hiccoughed with fright.

Mrs Tree was standing by the gate.

She had been staring down the street. Now she looked round. "Oh," she said, and blushed. "Good morning, Tom."

Tom? he thought distantly as he went forward in a swaying shuffle, the schoolboy heading for chastisement. "About last night."

Mrs Tree giggled. "You were really rather naughty. But Janet forgives you."

"She—Oh yes. Thank you . . . Janet." Tom was so overcome with his easy escape that he said, "How about having lunch with me?"

"Very well, Tom. Today?"

"Well, no." He touched his head. "Tomorrow."

"Fine."

He edged through the gateway and backed off. "I know a real good cafeteria downtown."

"That sounds thrilling, Tom. And perhaps we can talk more about your you-know-what."

"Eh?" said Tom, halting.

"You know." Janet glanced all around before leaning forward to hiss, "Your murderer."

Tom stared. "I told you?"

"Not his name. You were naughty about that too. Just his description."

That, thought Tom, was something at least. But how stupid could he be? Or (he amended) how drunk. "You mustn't breathe a word of it, Mrs—Janet."

"Oh, I shan't. And who was it he murdered, did you say?"

"I didn't say?"

"No. You told poor Janet hardly anything."

"Good. It's hush-hush." Quickly, so that he would not have to refuse to answer more questions, Tom turned and walked off with a wave and, "See you later."

By the time he had reached the common he had put his semi-indiscretion and Janet Tree out of his mind and was thinking about the earlier part of the eventful Saturday night. The talk in the pub, while accomplishing little, had made it plain that there was no mistake about the identity of Jack Partridge, alias Capstan, alias Armstrong. Not that there had been any doubt before. But it was satisfying to have it made final.

Now, for the first time, it occurred to Tom to wonder why. Why was he keeping this watch on Partridge?

Stopping under a tree to shade from the sun, which was growing hotter every day, Tom pondered the question. At once he realized there was nothing to ponder about. He had known all along. What he wanted was to wrap Partridge up

141

for the police, to hand him over all ready for trial, like a chicken trussed for the oven, to achieve a greatness that would be his for ever. A perfect wrapping-up meant of course a confession. And that's what he would get.

Tom strode on purposefully across the common.

Blackmail, thought Janet, now back in her parlour. Not a particularly pleasant-sounding word. But then, black things never were pleasant. Be that as it may, it was the solution to all her money problems, the ill wind that was going to blow her a great deal of good. She would not, naturally, overdo it. Her demands would not be ruinous. Even if they were, the guilty party would be happy to pay. They always did. She had read of it hundreds of times in books; the only difference being that the blackmailed was usually female, the heroine, a sweet girl with an unfortunate past. Well, this time it was the heroine's turn. All she needed was an identity.

Janet looked at the piece of paper on which, after her recent walk outside to look at the houses and refresh her memory, she had written the names of all the men in the street. Some names were incomplete. In one case she had only Charlie, in another she was not sure if it were Waterford or Watertown, in a third she had only the wife's Christian name, Regina.

Before going further she set out to solve these deficiencies, intrigued and thrilled by her task. The first was accomplished by telephoning the place where Charlie worked and asking to speak to "that tall boy, Charlie Whatsisname." The receptionist said, "Charlie Barton, you mean?" Janet put down the receiver.

It was simple to check on the second; she looked in the directory at everything following Water until she found a Gormon Lane address.

The third name she got by taking a cup, walking down the street to a woman she vaguely knew, asking for the loan of some sugar and during the ensuing chat repeating a remark supposedly made by "Mrs . . . Oh, what's she called, the house with the red gate?" "McNally."

In her parlour again, flushed with success, Janet wrote Tom's description of the murderer beside the list. Most names she crossed out, leaving seven. One was not actually of sturdy build, one was dark rather than medium and one had a pale face. However, since all were tall—and height could not be disguised—she was not taking any chances: the man might have lost weight, or dyed his hair or lightened his skin.

The next step, she thought, was how to reduce the seven to one, the right one.

This problem she worried with humming pleasure, as a puppy worries a shoe, while making herself a light lunch of poached eggs on toast. The thing was, none of them looked in the least bit villainous and none, to her knowledge, had ever done anything wrong. In fact, on the surface, all were highly respectable. Yet by the time she had finished eating she had found what she considered the one and only answer.

She would write to all seven.

That way she couldn't possibly not reach the right man. To six the letters would be meaningless, the seventh would understand. It was perfect. She congratulated herself on her shrewdness.

Now came the tricky part: how to phrase the missive. If she tried to say too much the murderer would see that she knew nothing, and the other recipients would be inclined to call in the authorities. She couldn't mention murder. She couldn't even mention crime. It had to be simple and ambiguous.

Getting more paper she began to scribble, writing and then crossing out sinister sentence after malign phrase. She enjoyed her search. It was like playing a word game. And she had hours to complete it in. If she posted the letters before the last Sunday pick-up at six, they would be delivered in the morning.

Finally she had the wording right. With a tingle of excitement she wrote seven times, on seven separate pieces of stationery, using longhand that sloped backwards instead of her normal forwards: *I know the truth about you. Meet me at 5 today outside the bank.*

She put the notes into envelopes, which she stamped and addressed. As she went to get her coat she wondered with amusement what the six innocent men would make of the letters.

7

The first person to open one of
Janet Tree's letters was not a tall man, well built and of
medium colouring, she was a small blonde.

Regina McNally, at twenty-seven, had a neat figure and
a pretty face, a dozen admirers and a constantly changing
rota of lovers, an invalid husband and a strong sexual appetite. The last two were incompatible. Hence the lovers.

When Regina had married some five years before, her
husband had been fit and virile. Two years later had begun
the illness which gradually reduced him to a pale ghost who
ate little, slept badly, felt permanently sorry for himself,
cultivated the invalid's faculty for invective, spent most of
his time in his aconjugal bed with an occasional sit on the
front lawn, a less occasional slow walk up the street.

Regina made no complaints, not even to herself. She
loved her husband and nursed him with care. Her desire she
sublimated for a year, turning away from stimulants as the
unhappy turn from laughter, exhausting herself with house-
work and other activities in which she insisted she was enormously interested.

One day, shopping in another part of Sydney, she allowed
herself to be picked up. The man took her to his flat and
began to make love to her. She was limply, unfeelingly sub-

missive. However: even though she had taken no enjoyment from the act, she agreed to meet the man again. She went home dazed, remorseful and determined.

She continued to meet the man and through him other men. She soon changed lovers, soon changed again. She had assignations two or three times a week, telling her husband she was going to language classes. She revelled in the sex and suffered the remorse, although the latter never kept her from the former. She was physically high, spiritually low.

The turnover in lovers was frequent, stemming mainly from the fact that Regina was overwilling, the predator, almost insatiable. Her men cut off the affair in fear of suffering that most dreaded blow to the masculine ego, infirmity. Sometimes Regina was the one to call it quits, this when she found the man or herself becoming involved beyond the venereal. She wanted no such involvement. She loved her husband.

Janet Tree's letter was opened by Regina because she it was who carried on the house's correspondence and paid the bills. She spared no thought for the name on the envelope; the message, which she read with shock, could have been meant for her alone. It was extortion. The writer wanted money, or services, in exchange for keeping the truth from her husband.

Regina spent the worst day of her life waiting for five o'clock, at which time she went to Dimple Hill's only bank. She strolled past, turned and strolled past again. On her third passing a man walked by and gave her a curious look, which she returned. He stopped farther along to glance back. Regina went toward him slowly. He looked in a shop window. She dawdled near, walked on. He followed. She stopped. He slowed. She looked at him with eyebrows raised.

Stopping beside her the man smiled and said, "Hello."

He was young and handsome and his smile was warm. Regina felt drawn toward him despite his intentions. "Hello," she said. "Are you the man I've been looking for?"

"Could be. How much?"

Regina wondered how he could smile so nicely when being so rotten. She said, "I don't know."

"You don't? Okay, I'll give you five dollars."

It took at least a minute for the truth to settle on Regina. She had made a mistake. This was not the right person. This one had taken her for a streetwalker. She was both injured and flattered.

"No?" the man was saying. "Six then."

Regina glanced along the street. There was no one in sight at the bank. She said, "I haven't got a room."

"I know a hotel in Paddington. We'll get a cab. Six dollars?"

"All right."

One week later, no more extortion letters having arrived, Regina purposely picked up one of her husband's cues to argue, argued, packed her things and left home. She took a small flat in King's Cross and became a prostitute, accepting only those men she found attractive.

She was happy, she felt no remorse; and until he died a few years later she went twice a week to a nursing home to visit her husband, whom she loved.

A stores manager and a bachelor, Ronald Jones-Grey was a thoroughly practical no-nonense man who had no room

147

in his life for jokes or cranks, and the letter was meant to be one or had been sent by the other. Ronald Jones-Grey burned the letter and never gave it a second thought.

"Greentrees" and "Everjoy" were Siamese twins, semi-detached houses which fought uselessly to escape from one another in the use of different paintwork and other cosmetics and the tall hedge between front gardens. The owners, Joe and Fred, both husbands and fathers in their middle thirties, both factory workers, had for years been carrying on a fight of the captured. Their only truly happy moments were when one could do the other metaphorically in the eye. They argued about the height of the hedge, about the noise, real or supposed or intentional, coming through the inner wall or outer windows, about the TV aerials on the shared chimney block, about who owned the posts of the back fence, about the throwing of garbage from one garden to the other, about the recovery of toys which had strayed into the wrong sandbox, about Fred's neglect of his frontage, which brought values down, about parties, about washing lines, about laughter too early in the morning. They endlessly threatened litigation and continually consulted lawyers, who told them not to be silly. Their children exchanged jeers, their wives heavy silence, themselves glares between arguments.

The most recent membrane of contention was Joe's apple tree. An upper branch hung over Fred's garden and Fred claimed that the fruit thereon belonged to him. Joe was derisive. Fred said okay so cut off the branch. Joe was even more derisive. Fred said *he* would cut off the branch, since it was trespassing. Joe said if Fred dared to touch one leaf of that branch *he* would be trespassing and what was more he, Joe, was going to pluck his apples whenever he felt like it. Oh, was he? Yes he bloody was. They both said they would see about that, they would just see.

On Monday morning Joe and Fred were short tempered with tiredness, having spent a restless night, each expecting to hear some stealthy action from the other. They read their unsigned letters at the same time, came to the same conclusion and went bursting outdoors at the same moment.

Meeting across the back fence they began their first and last fight. Although bitter and bloody, it was soon ended. They were dragged apart by their no-longer silent wives and their jeerless children.

It was the last straw. They sold their houses and moved to others in Dimple Hill.

After a time Joe and Fred met on the neutral ground of a social club, got to know one another, became firm friends and remained so for the rest of their lives.

Septimus Morgan was a schoolteacher who lived with his wife, two teenage daughters and his mother-in-law, which females cowered under his despotic rule.

When he read Janet Tree's letter at the communal breakfast table he smiled grimly, knowing by the childish writing that it had been sent by one of the boys in his class or perhaps by the class as a whole, a joint effort. He smiled his grimness rather than frowning it because he would enjoy bluffing and taunting the boys, individually and en masse, pretending he knew everything there was to know. He would drop hints about a handwriting expert, about fingerprints, about tracing types of stationery. He would give the dear boys hell.

Putting the letter away, Septimus Morgan continued his breakfast in a mood of unusual joviality, which made his female subjects rather frightened.

Charlie Barton was a twenty-four-year-old New Zealander, an unnaturally tall, skinny man with long floppy hair, pink-fresh face that looked seventeen, nervous gestures, and the general awkwardness which cripples those who have not matured enough to accept and forgive their fate, the awkwardness of apology.

He blushed a hundred times a day. He protested too much about the bother of having to shave so that no one would know that he never did. He was painfully pleasant to everyone. He laughed at the feeblest joke and at remarks he mistook for jokes. He was a willing prisoner of bores. He walked in a knock-kneed, bowed-headed stoop to reduce his impertinent height. He was eager and kind. He tripped over things.

His trouble had begun at school, where, suddenly it seemed, he was two feet taller than anyone else. He went around making fun of himself, which people thought peculiar in the extreme. They started to notice other strange characteristics. They noticed his laugh, high and frequent and somewhat wild, a laugh in which his eyes never participated for fear of not being able to see if his appreciation of the humour was well marked. Teachers and pupils said, "An odd one that." They observed his abnormal willingness to help, his dreamy expression when he thought himself alone, the way his hands would sometimes dance in front of him

150

while he was walking, and they told each other that he was a bit off. They saw his stoop and his blushes about nothing and his ready glare of a smile, and they shook their heads. They said he was definitely cracked.

Charlie aggravated the impression. After getting the vague feeling that he was being shunned, not only did he double his efforts in the traits that were suspect, he told a friend who was not a friend and who immediately passed the manic intelligence on to everyone else, told him to get a sample reaction, he told him the deepest secret of his heart: that he loved music, that it meant more to him than anything, that it created colours in his mind, that he saw all of life in terms of tone and tempo, that he hoped one day to be able to put this affinity to use. The story was flung around with joy, for Charlie was not in the school band, was indeed a duffer on the simplest musical instrument and always disagreed, apologetically, with the maths master who gave infrequent talks on musical appreciation. Charlie's lunacy was firmly established.

When this fact at last found its way into his naive mind Charlie was heartbroken. He was also afraid. Could it be true? Was not his father forever calling him a bloody fool and his mother telling him to get out of the way for God's sake and stop mooning around like an idiot? Did he not have the funniest ideas, the most curious dreams? Was it not strange that he preferred music and reading to playing cricket and soccer with the other boys?

But no, it was not true. He was simply in the wrong environment.

Charlie ran away from home, was brought back, ran away again and was brought back again. "There you are," people said. He was sent to another school. He was followed there by what he thought of as the Lie. He cried within him-

151

self and stayed within himself. He developed a facial tick. The music master told him he had no real feeling for music. When he argued, the master called him a head-case. He ran away.

On being brought back he was sent to another school—sneaked after by the Lie—and managed to stay on until leaving age, a nervous and frightened pine in a forest of taunting saplings. When his father asked what he wanted to do now, he murmured something about music. He was sent to a business college.

The college being in Aukland, six months passed before the Lie arrived. It was accepted at once. He was an odd one all right, that Charlie, with his ways of staring out of the window and humming and trying to help people who didn't need help. In the interests of the school, the principal asked him into his office for a chat and in what he considered the kindest possible way wondered aloud if Charlie had ever thought of seeing a psychiatrist. Charlie punched the principal as hard as he could and ran out, sobbing with humiliation and fear and at the pain in his broken finger.

Over the next five years, working at whatever came along, he moved from North Island to South, from several towns in Tasmania to more towns on the mainland, always, after a period of weeks or months, being chased on by the implacable Lie or by an acquaintance's remark, either snarled or laughed, following some oddity of a behaviour which had grown progressively more erratic.

For a year now Charlie had lived with a distant relative in Gormon Lane. He worked as a bookkeeper in a store whose owner, though wary of his employee, liked the low wage he was willing to accept. Charlie was close to being happy. He had no friends and his relative was old and deaf, but there were concerts, he had records, he had a radio. He dreamt joyfully of being a conductor who was five feet tall.

Janet Tree's letter arrived. Charlie read it with horror. His heart began its old familiar ache and the fear crawled around his bowels. Not pausing to question the letter or why its author should want a meeting, he hastily packed a bag and ran along the street with tears pouring down his face.

Three weeks later in Brisbane, a mate at the warehouse where he had that day found work told him jokingly but serio-faced that he must be out of his mind. This time Charlie did not run. He was through with running. He walked out of the warehouse, walked back to his lodgings, and hanged himself.

Back home, people said, "You see?"

8

"That's the post," said Mildred Partridge as a thump sounded from the direction of the front door. She got up from the table and left the kitchen.

Jack continued to eat—without interest, as had been his way of late, unless his mind happened to turn on food, when he would eat slowly and eagerly, savouring the sight and taste of every forkful, as if the meal were his first, or his last. At the moment it was merely a matter of shovelling in the ham and eggs to fill a void.

Mildred returned. She put three letters beside Jack's plate, sat in her place and opened her own mail. Jack glanced at the envelopes. Two were window-fronted, therefore bills. The third was addressed in longhand. The style was unfamiliar. He slit the envelope with a tine of his fork, took out a single sheet of paper, unfolded it and read:

I know the truth about you. Meet me today at 5 outside the bank.

Jack's first impulse was to smile, the wording seemed so silly, so melodramatic. But the impulse died aborning. As his eyes continued to glide forward and back across the message its childish Gothic was superseded by its significance. His reaction now was disbelief. He continued to read. He accepted. His final reaction was shock.

Mildred looked up. "Aunt Betty wants to—" She broke off, stared, leaned forward. "Jack, what's wrong?"

Slowly he raised his head and at the last moment his eyes from the repulsively fascinating paragraph. "Mm?"

"What's in that letter? You look upset."

He nodded, dragging his mind painfully from its involvement to the task of creating a suitable story. Folding the paper he returned it to the envelope, which he put into his pocket.

"Well?" asked Mildred. "Jack?"

"That man I sold a truck to the other night," he said. "He was told it was no good and he's calling the deal off."

Mildred looked relieved. "What's so upsetting about that?"

"Well, he says I was trying to cheat him."

Mildred gave an indignant snort. "You? Huh! You're the only honest car dealer in Sydney. He's got his nerve. What're you going to do about it? I know what I'd do. I'd . . ."

Jack let his wife ramble on; and when she had worked the car-dealer vein out he got her onto what Aunt Betty had to say. He encouraged his wife to talk to keep himself from thinking; yet on he thought, an underground operation.

As soon as he could without making his wife suspicious, he left the house. When he had reversed the car onto the road and was going forward he switched on the radio, loud; another delaying tactic.

He drove fast, far above the limit, screaming to a halt at traffic lights and surging away again a second before the green. He slowed, sweating, after he came close to hitting a warden at a school crossing.

At length he turned into a quiet road and stopped. Getting out he began to walk. His face was gravely alert as opposed to its recent expression of casual sadness. His hands were firmly pocketed, one clenched around the letter.

His shock had still not quite gone. The letter was the last thing he had expected. He had somehow become used to the idea that the situation would wander along in its same unresolving way. But this . . . *I know the truth about you.* Of course Tom Brady knew the truth, or rather the apparent truth. All doubt had been removed in the pub. So what was his game? There was only one answer to that. Blackmail. The dirtiest game of all. Something he would not have suspected of Brady. He seemed a decent type, if a moron. But the mind of a moron worked in mysterious ways its blunders to perform. Brady had hit upon something in an on-moment.

Jack's thoughts began to fluctuate between bitter acceptance and doubt. Tom Brady was not the kind of man for blackmail. Yet how could anyone tell? And then again, blackmail did not have to be behind the letter. Yes it did, there was nothing else that could be.

The main point was, however, what would he do should it turn out that blackmail it definitely was?

Jack decided to stop thinking. He glanced around, took out the letter, put it down and set it on fire. Returning to the car he drove off with the radio blaring. Despite himself, the underground movement fought on.

At the garage he spent the morning forcing conversations on people. He got in the way of his mechanics, interrupted the work of his repairs manager, startled the team at the petrol pumps by serving three customers and spoiled a potential buyer by overtalking about and overpraising the merits of a car. He answered the curious looks of his staff with the statement that he had felt lately that he was getting out of touch.

At mid-day he insisted on taking the sales manager out to lunch, choosing the busiest and noisiest restaurant he knew of. He talked during the whole meal. After lunch, not wishing to return to work, figuring that a repetition of his morning's behaviour might be too much, too odd, and be remembered later, he went to a bar and drank ginger ale while getting mixed up in a loud argument about cricket, of which he knew next to nothing. And at all times the underground was busy.

At four o'clock he drove back to Dimple Hill, as slow as the traffic would allow, killing time. Mildred was pleased that he had come home early; she was going to visit one of her daughters-in-law and now she could use the car. Jack was also pleased; with time growing short he no longer had the patience for distractions or the pretence of acting the part of a man without worries. He told Mildred to stay as long as she wanted, he would make his own tea. She left.

Jack strode around the house, in and out of rooms, until twenty-five minutes to five, when the wait became unbearable. He went outside, turned toward the nearest end of Gormon Lane and headed via the longest route for Dimple Hill's business district.

Once he nearly thought on the surface of Tom Brady and the mad solution. He shook his head and walked faster. It was too early yet for decisions.

At the shopping centre he went into the pub and made straight for the window. Farther along the street, at a crossroads, on a facing corner, stood the bank. No one waited or strolled there. The clock above the door said twelve minutes to five.

Jack turned to the bar, where only two men were drinking, outnumbered by the six bartenders who were busying themselves with preparations for the rush that would come when the business places began to close.

He ordered a beer, lowered its foam and returned to the window. He found himself tense.

The seconds ticked off at the rhythm of a funeral march. Every other minute Jack checked his wristwatch with the bank clock. Tom Brady stayed absent. Five o'clock languidly came and still no Brady, no one was standing by the corner building. Jack's tension started to slacken off. At five-fifteen he was sagging and tired.

He tasted his beer. It had gone warmly flat. Turning, surprised to find the room crowded—he had not been aware of the noise—he edged through to the bar, put aside his beer and ordered a brandy, which he took to a quiet corner.

He felt sick. It was the sickness of fear, for now he was giving cognizance to the thought which had long been murmured hissingly by the grey eminence of self-love who lurked at the periphery of his civilized mind.

Since blackmail it was, he knew, and worse—Brady intended playing a tantalizing game to reduce him to a willing, malleable wreck, ready to pay anything and go on paying to gain peace of mind—there was only one solution. He could not allow himself to be bled to ruin, his wife brought to penury and his children to shame.

Jack drained his brandy and faced the fact that he must kill Tom Brady.

The cafe had been a good choice. It was large and well packed with customers; moreover, its windows afforded a good view of the bank. These attributes, unfortunately, had gone to waste.

Janet Tree signalled a waitress for her bill with a sigh of annoyance. It was now five-thirty, time to go. She was annoyed with the stupid murderer for not having shown up and for having been forced to spend precious money on a plate of biscuits and three cups of coffee in order to fill in time and render unpeculiar the vigil of more than an hour.

After paying her bill and adding the minimal tip, Janet left the cafe and set off home. Sighing again, she thought that if only the murderer had turned up as expected everything would have been perfect. Not that she would have shown herself. Oh no. Nothing so foolhardy. She would have left him waiting there. The idea of the rendezvous was simply to find out which of the seven men on her list it was. Then she could have got to work. She would have written a less ambiguous letter, made her position quite plain and asked for a reply to be sent to . . . Well, she would have thought of somewhere, possibly Mr Beeker's pawnbroker's shop. She would have remained unknown to Mr X. Everything done by mail. A nice wad of cash arriving promptly on the first of every month.

A happy thought, but one never to be. Mr X refused to play. Which seemed odd in the extreme. Why had he not appeared at the bank? Even a murderer could not be maniac enough to misunderstand the implication in her letter, if he had received it.

Of course! she told herself, brightening. That was the answer. She had missed out the right man, had not included him among the short list of seven. It was quite feasible that Tom, being as he was somewhat in his cups, had given an incorrect description. Should she not tackle him again on the subject, in a roundabout way? He wouldn't mind. He had not minded last evening when they talked in the hall, he had merely repeated in the sweetest tone of voice that his work was secret and highly confidential and he was not at liberty to discuss its smallest detail. After all, they were quite close now. Today they had lunched together downtown, chatting away like the oldest of friends, when she had told of the other boarders' departure without mentioning the reason. Yes, quite close. Intimate, you could say. Why, he had even talked of marriage. His own marriage, to be sure. But marriage. No, Tom wouldn't mind if she dropped a hint or two about the identity of the murderer.

Tom Brady had finally got everything worked out for getting a confession from Jack Partridge. Already he had gone through the act a dozen times; now he was about to go through it again. He wanted to have it down pat, move-perfect. When he got Partridge up here in his room, after a day or two, after he had talked with him a few more times to remove suspicion, everything had to go as smooth as a swallowed oyster.

Tom stood in the centre of the floor, gave his throat a good clearing, and thought: Right. He is coming up the stairs. First flight, second flight. He is knocking on the door. Knock knock.

Tom strode to the door and pulled it open. "Come in, Jack, come in. A pleasant evening, eh? Ha ha."

Yes, it was a pleasant evening, Partridge says as he steps inside.

Tom closed the door and made a gesture toward the conversation ensemble of two chairs and low table. "Won't you . . ." He paused, frowning. What if Partridge chose the wrong place to sit, ignoring the armchair and taking the upright chair, on which he would be more difficult to handle, could in fact pick it up with him and move about?

Taking the seat of debased value Tom put it against the wall, turned, gestured again and said, "Do sit down, Jack old man."

Partridge says thank you and sits.

Tom stepped swiftly to the bed (not part of the act this), got a pillow and laid it upright against the armchair's backrest. Movements slow once more, he said to the pillow: "It's better, sitting, eh? Ha ha."

Partridge says yes it is more comfortable sitting.

"How about a drink? Or a cigarette?" If neither of these, Tom thought, then: "Well, if you will excuse me for one second, I shall close the wardrobe door, which is standing open, as you might have noticed as you came in."

Partridge agrees that it would be better to have the wardrobe door closed.

Tom stepped behind the easy chair. His movements returned to swift, now greatly part of the act. From under his jacket, where it had been lying snug against his belly, he pulled a rope formed from a scarf tied to a bathrobe cord. Holding an end in each hand, as though about to skip, he flung the rope over the chair back and across the pillow.

Partridge asks what the hell is this.

Tom shot to one knee and tied the rope ends together.

Partridge, secured across the arms and chest, curses softly.

Tom rose, all calmness, turned to the wardrobe, reached inside and made a flicking motion with his finger, simulating the switching on of the tape recorder which he would buy as soon as possible.

He strolled to front his prisoner, drawing from an inside pocket a foot-long evil-looking piece of iron—he had picked it up the day before on the common. Tapping the iron in the palm of one hand, frowning down sternly at the pillow, he said:

"Now, Partridge, what have you got to say for yourself?"

Partridge opens his eyes wide with fear.

There came a knock on the door.

Tom bobbed in alarm.

Mrs Tree's voice called, "It's only me, Tom. Janet."

Tom hurled back, "Just a second." It took him at least thirty to untie his rope, put it and the iron on the bed and cover them with the pillow. "Come in."

Janet entered with a tray. "I thought I'd bring you up a nice cup of tea. And I'll join you, if you don't mind."

"Of course I don't mind," said Tom, recovered from his fluster. As always, he was charmed by this young woman's attention and kindness. He had still not got over how nice she had been about his drunken performance. She had graciously forgiven him when he had not even forgiven himself—at least, not for his big-mouthedness. He thought what fine people they were, the Australians. Salt of the earth.

He said, "You spoil me."

"And why not?" She put the tray on the table and drew forward the upright chair for herself. "There we are. It's two sugars, isn't it, Tom?"

When they were settled and had exchanged steam-blinked glances over the rims of their cups, Tom asked sympathetically if she had done anything yet about filling the two vacant rooms. As before, at lunch, she told of the local drawbacks, ending with:

"It's such a problem, money."

"It is, it is."

"What a pity that people have to bother with such things."

"Well, I've had the problem all my life, to be truthful."

"I've been lucky, I suppose. My parents were comfortably off, rich for all I know. Certainly there never seemed to be money worries. Whatever I wanted I always got. Mummy and Daddy always said it was my right."

"Sound like good parents."

"They were. They doted on me. I was their only child. I don't think they were too happy with the idea that I had to grow up. And really, I was still a child when I ran away to get married."

"They wouldn't be too happy about that either, eh?"

"Very *un*. But the point is, again I was lucky, because against all odds—I knew nothing about him, background and so on—my husband turned out to be fairly well-to-do."

Janet went on to talk of her brief marriage. Tom thought it odd how matrimony kept creeping into their conversations. He wondered . . . But Janet was talking. He listened. And as he listened, Tom found himself irked that she should be extolling the virtues of her late husband.

". . . unfortunately he spent most of his cash money during the three weeks we were together, leaving little else besides this house. Or I should say, *I* did the spending. He spent nothing on himself. His joy was in giving. Every afternoon he would hand me a large heap of dollars—pounds in those days—and send me off in a taxi to buy myself something. Anything. His only stipulation was that the purchase be expensive and ridiculous. Then I'd go back to the hotel and have to show off what I'd bought. If it were frivolous enough he would be delighted with me and then we'd, um"—Janet flushed, coughed, and finished in a mumbled—"we'd have a good laugh."

"Yes, money's a problem," said Tom, wanting to get away from the subject of the gallant, wealthy husband and seeing with pleasure that Janet was obviously embarrassed by having spoken of him at length.

Janet nodded and sipped her tea. She put down the cup and nodded again. "Talking of money," she said. "I've been wondering, you know, about your murderer."

Tom couldn't see what money had to do with murder, but he put this aside to hold up a warning finger and say, "As I told you, I'm afraid I'm not able to discuss the matter."

"Yes, and I wouldn't dream of getting you to tell me anything you shouldn't. I just wondered if you'd got the description right, that's all."

"Quite right, thank you."

"And the age was, er . . . ?"

Uncomfortable, Tom looked around and found escape in remembering the lack of connexion. He asked, "What has this to do with money?"

"Well," she said, drawing out the word as long as a yawn, "I'll tell you. More tea?"

Tom shook his head. He watched uneasily as Janet, humming, poured tea into a cup, added sugar and milk, stirred with care, then pushed the readied drink away.

"I was thinking," she said, "how someone could make money out of this."

"Oh?"

"Yes. Your murderer, your Mr—what did you say his name was?"

"I didn't."

"Well anyway, Mr X, who, it appears, is six feet tall with—"

"What about the money?"

Janet clucked her tongue, folded her arms and leaned forward. "If a person told Mr X that he had to pay so much a month if he wanted his secret kept I'll bet he'd be glad to do it."

"Oh well. Very likely. But you couldn't do that."

"Why not?"

"Well, you just couldn't."

"But that sort of thing's done all the time."

"But you know what it is, don't you? What it's called."

"Yes," she said proudly. "Blackmail."

"Well then."

"Well what?"

He looked at her as a parent looks at a catechizing child, fondly yet with exasperation. "It's illegal."

"Oh phoo. How silly."

"And besides, it's not right."

"Why not?"

Tom's look became helpless. "Well . . . well . . ."

"Why isn't it right, Tom?"

He swallowed. "Because it's not honest."

"Oh," she said. "Honest."

He began to sigh with relief, catching back the sigh when Janet went on, "What's honesty got to do with it? Murder's wrong, isn't it?"

"Er—"

"I mean, if a person's got a secret, why shouldn't he pay to have it kept? Simple commerce, it seems to me. Furthermore . . . Is that my telephone?"

"Yes," said Tom, after which he heard faintly the ringing from below.

Janet frowned. "Who can that be, I wonder."

"Maybe someone about the rooms."

"I haven't put an ad in the paper yet."

"Well, you never know."

"True. Excuse me, please." She got up and left the room.

166

Tom allowed his sigh of relief to seep out in all its long, plaintive length. Putting a hand to his damp brow he mused that women were the damndest creatures. They were incapable of understanding the simplest logic. In Janet's case, however, there was something touchingly childlike in her innocence, in her ignorance of the nasty ways of the world.

Tom smiled. The next second he returned to gravity as he realized that soon Janet would return and he still didn't know how to explain why blackmail was not honest.

"Coo-ee!" called Janet. "It's for you."

He went out to the stairhead. "Me? Who is it?"

"He wouldn't give his name."

Tom shrugged and went down. In the parlour Janet handed him the telephone receiver, took herself into the kitchen and closed the door. Tom said into the mouthpiece, "Hello?"

"That you, Tom? Jack here. Jack Partridge."

"Ah," said Tom, surprised. With a glance toward the kitchen he lowered his voice. "Well, how are you, Jack?"

"Fine. Been a nice day, mm? Ha ha."

"Yes it has. Very nice."

"Look, Tom, I was wondering if we could meet this evening for a little talk."

Tom smiled. Partridge was playing right into his hands. "Why, I think that's a great idea, Jack. It's about time we had a talk."

"Good. Where shall we meet?"

"Why not come here, to my room?"

"No, I couldn't do that, Tom. You know the situation as well as I do. We'll have to meet in secret."

"Naturally. That's what I mean. It'll be quite secret here. I'm the only lodger in the house now. And anyway," continued Tom with a flash of inspiration, "I can't go out, can't walk very far. Gout y'know."

"Gout?"

"It comes on me every time I have too much to drink. And you know how much I had the other night, don't you, Jack? Ha ha."

"What about the landlady there?"

"Make it late enough, say ten, and she'll be in bed. I'll be waiting to let you in, so you won't have to ring. No one'll see you come and go."

A pause, until: "All right. Ten o'clock. But if there's anyone else around I shan't come."

"I'll be quite alone, Jack. My oath."

"Okay. See you at ten."

"See you at ten." Tom put down the receiver delicately, like a cat unmouthing its kitten. He hunched his shoulders and placed his hands together in a tight grip, squeezing over his satisfaction. Everything was set.

Janet looked into the room. "Finished, Tom?"

"Yes, thanks. It was a pal of mine. Wants to know if I'll meet him at once. So I'll be off now."

Although pleased to note that Janet looked disappointed, Tom was more concerned with the thoughts of buying a tape recorder. He glanced at the mantel clock, said a polite good afternoon and hurried out.

Jack Partridge still sat in his hallway beside the telephone. He was not happy about the meeting place. It made his plan doubly dangerous. But there was no choice. The plan had to be gone through with while he was hot in his decision. If he delayed until Brady was fit to go out, he might waver, which would be fatal.

Then why hadn't he arranged to pick Brady up in his car? And should he do so?

Jack basted the idea carefully with thought before turning it down. He himself could slip into the house and if he were seen would most likely not be recognized; with a car it would be different, him waiting, Brady limping out. If his face wasn't seen, his car was known. And since they were meeting supposedly for a simple talk, Brady would think elaborate precautions peculiar.

Now Jack wondered if it were true that the other lodgers had left. It seemed odd that they should both leave so suddenly after such a long stay. Yet why should Brady lie? If he were suspicious of his visitor's intentions he would be more likely to impress upon him the fact that there were other people in the house, potential witnesses. So he was not suspicious. He was looking forward to a chat about a financial settlement. The house it was.

Jack lifted the telephone receiver and dialled the home of one of his sons. He asked to speak to Mildred. He told her that as he had to go out on business she should stay where she was for supper and come home as late as she liked.

Leaving the house he went into his garage, to the work bench along one side. Behind, on the wall, were tools and implements stuck in leather pouches. From one of these he took an ice pick, its blade of super-slenderness dark with rust. He put the handle in a vise and filed on the blade until it was shiny. Out of a can he scooped a fingerload of heavy car grease, which he spread on the blade from point to hilt. Last, he wrapped newsprint loosely around the whole pick and put it into his inside breast pocket.

The ice pick would be used in a method of killing he had heard of somewhere, long ago. You drove the weapon swiftly in and out of the heart. The grease sealing the wound, there was no blood. There was hardly even a wound. In a man of Tom Brady's age and overweight, death would be attributed to a heart attack. Only a highly mistrustful and thorough police surgeon would find the minute hole in the chest.

Back in the house, in the front room, Jack sat at a writing desk, arranged paper before him and poised a pen. He was about to write a confession. It would get things straight in his own mind in addition to its true purpose: a diversion necessary to the killing of Tom Brady.

He began at the meeting with Carlotta in a Brighton dance hall. He wrote steadily, finding that the story came without trouble and that there was a surprising amount of gratification in putting it all down. He wrote for an hour, reaching the night he had smashed his car into a wall, at which point he broke off to get himself a bottle of beer.

As he sipped, he let his mind play over the rest of the story. It had been so strange, he thought, lying in that bed . . .

"You're much better today," said the doctor, his white coat gleaming like a light in the darkened room. "It's not a bad concussion."

"It had a bad effect though."

"Yes, it did," the doctor said with a faint smile.

For the first time in his three hazy days as a patient in the Basingfield Cottage Hospital, Jack made a close examination of the doctor. Placid of eye and middle-aged, his military moustache and upright bearing and overall neatness gave the impression of a man who was given to rules and the all correct, not to casual frivolity. Why then did he smile? Did he have some knowledge that Jack did not?

"You seem pleased, Doctor."

"As I just said, you're much better today."

Jack asked, "And you're sure there were no papers anywhere, even in the car?"

"Positive," said the doctor briskly, as if disliking the idea, whereupon Jack realized that his smile came from professional pleasure. It could not be often that they got such an interesting case in this little country hospital.

The doctor asked, "Remembered anything since last night?"

"No. It's a bit scary, all this."

"I can imagine. However, we'll soon get you right. What's the expression? As right as . . . ?"

"I don't know."

"It doesn't matter. Don't try to force anything."

Shifting his legs into a more comfortable position, Jack asked, "What's it all about, this loss of memory thing?"

"Well, I'm not a specialist, of course, and that's what we might have to do eventually, call in a specialist, but I have been doing some reading on the subject since you came to us."

"Yes?"

The doctor moved to the foot of the bed and leaned against the rail. "Amnesia, or fugue, can be caused psychologically, that is to say self-caused. A person reaches an hysterical climax in a life which is to him intolerable or shameful, and goes into shock. He refuses to remember because he doesn't want to, though he isn't aware of this refusal."

171

"I see."

"But in your case it seems to be purely physical—the bash on the head—which is nice and healthy. Some amnesias are partial, in the sense of being limited to one particular event or period. Then there's amnesia of speech, being mute. The extreme cases are those in which the patient forgets everything, completely everything. He can't walk or even sit up by himself. He's a baby. Luckily, your case isn't so extreme. At least you can talk."

"But I don't know if I can walk."

"You can. It's just that we prefer you to lie still." The doctor paused, as if taken by a thought. He asked, "Tell me, does it embarrass you to use the bedpan and bottles?"

"Embarrass me? Why, no. Should it?"

The doctor gave a shrug. "Just curious," he said. "Well, I'll get along. If your headache comes back, tell the nurse, she knows your pills."

"You're all being very good to me."

Waving this away, the doctor said, "I've told the police you're fit to receive visitors now. They'll be in to see you when they have time. They're not in a hurry. I gather there's no question of criminal negligence—bad corner that, where you crashed. In fact, I dare say you're more interested in seeing them than they are in seeing you."

"Why's that?"

"They should be able to trace you to a name. Which might do the trick. A jolt is probably all you need. A face, a place from your past."

"I see."

When the doctor left, Jack wondered why he had answered "I see." He did not see. Nor had he understood many of the other things the doctor had said, especially the long words. Criminal negli- something. What did it mean?

172

He raised and examined his hands. As before, they told him nothing, the same as with his face when the nurse had given him a mirror.

Growing tired of the constant worrying, Jack closed his eyes and dozed off. He awoke when a nurse came in to change his head bandage. Later she returned to spoon-feed him beef tea. Still later another nurse came to read aloud a list of first names, after each one asking, "Well?" or "No?" When she started on a list of towns Jack told her his head was beginning to ache. She left, he slept.

He next awoke to the sound of the door opening. A voice said, "Visitor for you, sir." The door closed and he was looking at a woman. She was strikingly pretty. Her clothes, after the plainness of hospital whites, were more gorgeous in colour than the flower picture on the wall.

"Hello," he said.

She came to the bed, sat on it close to his hip and gave him an intense, searching look, covering every part of his face. At last she spoke, and he noted with amusement that the end of her nose wiggled.

She said, "Jack, is it true you've lost your memory?"

"Jack? Is that my name?"

She nodded. "It's true then."

"Yes, it's true. So you know me?"

"I know you, darling."

"Good. I'm glad somebody knows me."

"My poor darling," she said, and leaning down kissed him full on the mouth.

When he freed himself (he was not sure that he liked being kissed), he asked, "Are you my mother?"

It was a surprise when she laughed, though it was an odd sort of laugh, harsh. "Haven't lost your sense of humour, have you, darling?"

"Who are you, please?"

"I'm your wife."

Jack took this in slowly. It seemed quite acceptable. "You are my wife," he said.

"Yes, darling. Your own Carlotta."

"Carlotta. That's a nice name."

"Angel." She kissed him again. Now he found it less unpleasant. He thought he might even get to like it after a while.

Breaking off the kiss but staying close she said in a low, urgent voice, "Now, listen, darling. There's no time to lose. I told them outside that you might be my cousin. That's why they let me in. I gave them a false name."

"Huh?" said Jack. He didn't understand a thing she was saying.

"Darling, we've got to hurry. Thank God I found you before the police discovered your identity. They're looking for you all over the country."

Jack shook his head in bewilderment. This sounded fantastic. "Me? The police are looking for me?"

"Your name's Royce, Jack Royce. That means nothing to you?"

"Nothing," he said worriedly. "Why are the police looking for me? Have I done something wrong?"

"My poor sweet darling. You really don't know? Well yes, you've done something wrong, to understate it. You're the most wanted man in Britain."

Jack stared. He began to feel frightened. He licked his lips and asked, "But what have I done?"

"I don't think I'd better tell you now. You've had shocks enough."

"What will they do to me when they catch me?"

"That doesn't bear thinking about. But they won't catch

you if we're clever." Her voice became more urgent: "The first thing is, we've got to get you out of here!"

The next ten minutes were like a game in the dark, part silly, part alarming, and with everything a mystery. Jack was hissingly urged on and nervously helped to get into his clothes, which were found in a closet. He followed Carlotta out of the window and at a crouch along beside the building to a place where cars were parked, into one of these and off with a roar.

Holding tightly to his seat as Carlotta took the car wailingly around a corner, Jack asked, "Where are we going?"

"Home," she said.

Home was a flat, palatial and luxurious in comparison to his room at the hospital. They stayed there one night, a night for Jack of amazing discovery, some nausea and a deal of physical thrills. The following morning they packed suitcases and left for a hotel, where they also stayed only one night, moving to another hotel the next day, another the next, keeping up the daily move for two weeks, until Carlotta rented a flat in the name of Capstan and returned the car to a hire firm.

During their travels Carlotta had her hair cut short and got Jack a pair of dark glasses, bought him presents of a wristwatch and a diamond ring, taught him to drink and told him why he was wanted by the police.

The charge was murder. He had killed his best friend. The motive: jealousy. Thinking his friend was trying to win Carlotta away from him he had bought a gun and blown his brains out. On hearing this Jack had fainted. When he came round he shivered so badly that Carlotta had to call a doctor, who gave him a sedative. It was days before he calmed down to a steady fear.

Slowly Jack acquired a remembered past. He remembered last week and the hospital; then last week, the week before, and the hospital; then last month, and the hospital.

There were moments of delight, periods of gloom. He had the feeling that it was not right that he should be ordered about, but once when he refused to clean her shoes she said if he were a naughty boy she would turn him over to the police; he cleaned her shoes. The fear was always there. It haunted his dreams and caused a shrivelling inside him at the sight of a uniform.

Yet, despite the fear, the gloom and the subjugation, or because of them perhaps, he grew rapidly in sophistication and knowledge. He learned how to hurt, how to love, how to live.

They went to theatres, concerts, races, exhibitions, pubs, gaming clubs and night clubs. Often, almost every time they were out, Carlotta would grab his arm and hiss that someone who knew them was around. They would leave wherever they were and run. On these occasions, Jack, drenched with fear, always had the suspicion that Carlotta was enjoying herself.

They chased pleasure in every waking moment. And, when Jack's confidence grew, they fought.

9

The hall of "West Wind" lay in a state of dusk. Although no light came from beneath the doors of Janet Tree's parlour or bedroom, a glow did float feebly down from the top landing, while a street lamp filtered its rays through the pebbled glass in the upper half of the front door.

This window it was that Tom Brady had his eyes fixed upon, waiting for a shadow. He had positioned himself midway down the bottom flight of stairs, from where he could make a safe retreat should danger sound from the bedroom. The iron was in his pocket, the rope under his coat.

Too, everything above stood in readiness for the act. The straight chair had been put back against the wall and behind the ajar wardrobe door waited a transistorised tape recorder, which he had finally managed to get by rousing the owner of a closed shop from his rear living quarters and which he had spent two hours in conquering.

He looked at his watch. Ten minutes to go. Already he had waited fifteen, coming down early because, you never knew, his watch might be wrong. Now he was starting to ache with tension. His feet were cold and the step edge was biting into his back. His mouth, lungs and nerves groaned in chorus for a cigarette.

177

He wondered if, since there were ten minutes left, he should go up to his room, relax and have a smoke. He could keep watch from the window and when . . . No, the time was too close; Partridge might come while he was on his way up, or down, find no one waiting, and go away.

Sighing, Tom averted his thoughts from the idea of smoke and relaxation as a woman might avert her eyes from fornicating dogs, not out of distaste but the fear of being seen watching. He sat still and cheered himself by dwelling on the future, post-confession. Fame and fortune, that's what he would have. Picture in the papers, name a household word, asked to speak at dinners, join clubs, open bazaars, appear on television, given the keys of Sydney, paid to endorce commercial products. People would point him out in the street. He would be asked for his autograph. He would carry a pocketful of cents to hand out to children. He might even get married. He—

Was that a shadow?

It was.

Small, at the bottom of the window, the shadow moved raggedly across the pimpled glass, came halfway up and stopped. A creak: the gate. The shadow moved again, grew. It grew until the window was filled.

Rising, Tom went daintily down the stairs and along to the door, which he opened with the greatest care, his mouth held stiffly wide, bottom teeth bared.

He whispered, "That you, Jack?"

The answer was barely audible. "Yes."

"Come in."

"There's no one else about?" asked Jack, stepping softly inside.

"No one. Mrs Tree's asleep."

While not wishing to ask more questions, knowing they

could rouse suspicion, Jack was unable to resist, "You haven't told anyone about me, have you?"

Tom turned from closing the door. "No, honestly." He assured himself that this was not a lie, for Janet really knew nothing. "Follow me."

They tiptoed upstairs, Tom, remembering in time that he was supposed to have gout, putting one foot down flat with an accompanying sway of body. They breathed out heavily when in the safety of the bedroom. In a normally pitched voice, Tom said, "Pleasant night, eh?"

Jack nodded. He stood in the centre of the room, looking down. He looked down because he wanted to avoid looking at his host. He had no desire to remember him too well.

When asked if he would like a cigarette, Jack shook his head. He did the same when offered a drink. Gritting his teeth, he cursed Brady for being so hospitable.

Tom pointed to the armchair. "Won't you sit down?" He was surprised when, instead of answering or moving, Partridge, his eyes lowered as if in shame, reached into his pocket and brought out a folded manuscript. He put it on the table and said:

"I want you to read this."

"What is it?"

"My confession."

Tom didn't try to stop his mouth from sagging. "Your what?"

"My confession."

"You mean it?"

"Read it and see."

"But I don't understand."

"What's to understand?" asked Jack gruffly. "Why d'you think I wanted to see you?"

"I really don't know."

"Read it."

Bewildered yet elated and at the same time vaguely disappointed, Tom turned to the wardrobe and partially hid himself behind its door while pulling the rope from under his jacket. He returned to the table, picked up the sheets of paper and sat in his armchair. "Well!" he said, bewilderment winning.

"Read it."

Unfolding the papers, Tom read, *I first met Carlotta in Brighton. She was at a dance with another man and I was with another girl.* After a glance up, he read on.

Jack brought an upright chair forward and sat. He crossed his knees then they began to tremble. Brady, he saw, seemed to be getting suitably engrossed. Jack realized that although the confession had taken a long time to write, it would not take long to read; already three of the dozen pages had been turned over. Tom Brady had to be killed now, at once.

Jack stood up—Brady read on. Jack took two quiet steps toward the door—Brady read on. Jack circled to the back of the armchair—Brady read on.

The position was good. With an overarm sweep he could strike in the right place, that spot near the breastbone where lapel, sweater and tie intersected, while not having to see Brady's face when he did strike.

So all right, he told himself, strike.

He brought out his roll of newspaper, hand trembling so much the paper rattled, peeled off the newsprint and pushed it noisily into his pocket. Brady read on.

Jack gripped the ice pick in his right hand. He could hear the throb of blood in his ears. Eyes tight, he glared down at the striking place. He was badly frightened. Slowly he raised the weapon, stretching his arm to its full length.

She was a sweet girl, Tom read, *with hair like golden sunshine and those big eyes, blue ones, that children have and her lips were as sweet as a rose. After Carlotta she was more than a treat. She was an angel.*

Jack's raised arm trembled with its stiffness and with his emotion. Sweat stood out on his upper lip like scattered spawn. He shot angry eyes at the weapon hand, as if to command it to smash down. It stayed shakily put. He gasped and sweated and urged himself, do it do it.

Brady turned over another page. There were not many left.

It occurred to Jack how incredibly fantastic the situation was. The man sitting quietly reading, a man he hardly knew and didn't hate, with himself standing here trying to commit murder and making what seemed a monstrous amount of noise with his gasping and shaking.

To make himself act he tried another tactic, shock, the slap to an hysteric, by thinking: I will do it . . . NOW!

His arm stayed up.

She had ruined me with Sally, Tom read, *telling her all those vicious lies. And Sally was the nicest thing that had ever happened to me in my life. The mess at the gatehouse flat was nothing compared to this. Sally, Carlotta and my employer, they kept running through my head as I drove faster and faster.*

Jack made a weak attempt of telling himself that Tom Brady was a criminal, a blackmailer, a worker of the lowest and slimiest game of all, that there was no one in the world to care if he lived or died, that he deserved to die.

It was no good. He couldn't do it. Saggingly he brought back the ice pick and put it into his pocket. Drooped at his side, his arm began to ache.

Dizzy, still trembling, he returned to the chair, sat down

181

and leaned forward, forearms on knees. He felt so tired he could not make the effort of wiping the sweat from his face.

A few more minutes and Tom came to the last paragraph: *The arguments grew frequent. Several times a day Carlotta would do or say something that could be made into a quarrel. If I didn't pick up the challenge, she sneered. If I did, the fight was on. And the fights grew more vicious.*

Thoughtfully and gravely Tom tapped the pages together, folded the script and placed it on the table. The confession was incomplete, but no doubt the rest would be coming now verbally. Perhaps in the form of a plea? A request that the death be classed as justifiable homicide?

Tom looked across at his slumped guest. He felt disturbed. He was not sure why. Unless it stemmed from the fact that in the confession Jack Partridge came across as a decent man, someone who always tried to do the right thing. Which, of course, could have been the intention. Anyone could make himself sound a great bloke, especially if there was no one to give the other side of the story. But there again, it fitted with what had been learned about Partridge from friends and colleagues.

Tom cleared his throat. Partridge looked up, lifting his head as slowly as though it wore a leaden crown. His face was drawn. For a moment he seemed not to know where he was: then his eyes blinked off their film and he nodded.

Tom asked, "This Carlotta, she's the one? The, um, victim?"

"Yes."

"She sounds like a real bitch."

"She was," Jack said, moving upright, changing from an elbow rest to a hand rest. His fingers gripped into his thighs as he tried to speak as forcefully, as earnestly as possible.

He felt it was important. "A complete bitch. Rotten through and through. Believe me. Please."

Tom believed. He said as much.

"She was rotten in a thousand ways, big and small. In things I don't want to write about or speak of or even think of. In any case, some of them are unbelievable. She was evil."

"I believe you."

"Thank you."

"But did she deserve to die?"

Jack shook his head. "No one deserves to die. People like that should be kept out of society."

"Yet she did die."

"Let me tell you the rest of it."

"Yes."

Jack paused to wipe a foreknuckle across his mouth. He said, "Our last fight, it started in a night club. I can't remember what it was about. Maybe because I wanted to go home and she didn't. She never wanted to go home. Unless she felt more like sex than drink. We argued till the club closed and all the way to the flat. Inside we really exploded. It was our worst fight, though I was no match for Carlotta. She was always offensive, I defensive. This time, after the screaming and throwing, she grappled with me, trying to get at my eyes with her fingernails. Finally she bit my hand till the blood ran.

"That's when I reached what they call the breaking point. I picked up the poker."

Jack ran a trembly hand over his new-sweating face. He had never allowed himself to go over this moment before. Only nightmares had kept it alive.

"Yes?" urged Tom, leaning forward.

"She, Carlotta, she screamed at me to remember who I

183

was. But I couldn't. I could only remember last month, the month before that, and the hospital."

"Yes?"

"So I killed her."

Tom leaned back. Even while gratified to hear and possess the final admission, he felt shocked at the statement, so powerful in significance yet so simply offered. His hands came together and his fingers began to intertwine.

"It was then," Jack said, "when she had fallen to the floor, dead and bloody, that my memory came back. It was terrible, horrible."

Tom clucked his tongue in sympathy.

Jack forced himself away from the picture of blood. "I remembered everything from the past, and how Carlotta had been lying to me about being wanted by the police. But that had been a prophetic lie. I'd be wanted now. I got out. That's when I saw you downstairs."

"Yes."

Jack took a deep breath. "It was only later that I realized I was innocent."

Tom sat up. "Innocent?"

"Yes, without guilt."

"You—"

"I killed Carlotta, yes, was the cause of her death, but I didn't commit murder. Murder is a crime, and I was too young to know about that."

"What're you saying?" asked Tom, his face screwed up.

Jack became earnest again, leaning forward gripping his knees. He spoke with care. Here was the crux of the matter and he had to get it right. If Brady understood, others would understand. Others and the police.

"Don't you see," he said. "I was a child. I remembered

184

nothing of the background, environment, teaching, learning, experience, the things that make us into responsible citizens. All of us are born savages. We have to be taught, trained. I struck out as a child strikes out, with its natural inborn instinct for self-protection. The only difference was, I had the strength of a man, whereas it's rare that a child, unless it has the right instrument, kills the playmate who hits it or steals its toy, though it does happen. And it is not murder. Murder is an act of responsibility. Do you understand me?"

Tom had sunk slowly back in his chair. He nodded. Understand he did. Jack Partridge was not guilty.

"My act was a reflex," Jack went on, "born of nature, not of civilized malice. Each and every one of us is capable of killing if for one brief moment we're driven to a rage of forgetfulness, so torn with emotion we are no longer our true adult selves. And in my case the amnesia was not a fleeting thing, it had been there for months. Sure you understand?"

"Yes," murmured Tom, feeling adrift, without purpose. He had been robbed of his drive.

"I'm not a criminal. Certainly not a murderer. In fact I tried to murder you while you were reading." He showed the ice pick. "I couldn't do it."

Tom gaped. He felt more adrift than ever, as if he no longer had any part in the proceedings, was a mere observer.

"Now," said Jack. "The thing is, do you accept my explanation? Do you believe me, and believe *in* me?"

Tom roused himself. "Well yes. Yes, I suppose I do."

"You're sure?"

"Well, yes."

"Absolutely?"

"Yes."

Jack sighed. "Good." He rose heavily to his feet. He was filled with the ache and strain of his release from fear; the fear of tonight's attempt at killing, of the recent days and of the past thirty years. Brady had understood. Others would too. He would now force to consummation the inevitable which he had accepted a week ago.

"Where're you going?" asked Tom.

"To the police."

"What!"

"I'm going to give myself up."

"Wait a bit, wait a bit." Tom put a hand to his head. Things were moving too fast. A minute ago Partridge had explained why he was innocent, now he said he was going to the police. Tom asked:

"Why give yourself up?"

"To get everything straightened out. I've lived with this too long."

"You can't do it."

"I know, it'll spoil your game."

"My game? No no, I'm not interested in your confession." Neither understood the other's meaning, and neither cared. Jack walked to the door. "This is going to make me feel happy again."

Tom pushed himself up. "Hold on. You're putting your neck in a noose." He stared at Partridge, horrified by the picture evoked by his statement. Here was a man, completely innocent, a decent good-living man, about to throw everything away when there was no need. Tom also felt in a smaller way that this was unfair, Partridge taking away his big chance and then going to the police anyway. "You don't know what you're doing."

"Yes, I do," said Jack. He opened the door and went out.

186

Tom followed hurriedly, across the landing, down the stairs. "They'll never believe you."

"You believed me."

"I'm different. I know you. And I don't go by rules and regulations like the law. To them, murder is murder."

"They'll understand."

"No," said Tom, putting a hand on Jack's shoulder as they turned on the first landing. "I can't let you do it."

Jack shook off the hand and went on down. "I've made my mind up."

"Look, you didn't murder that woman. But justice is black and white. They don't admit anything grey."

"They'll understand."

"Never. They'll pull your case to pieces. They'll laugh in your face."

One behind the other, Jack striding, Tom taking short quick nervous steps, they went along the hall, outside and down the path to the street. Tom trotted at Jack's side. He was growing frantic. He believed in Partridge as he had never believed in anyone. Partridge had suddenly become a symbol of Right. If the main purpose of Tom's recent life had been amputated, there was a lesser one here: he could still try to prevent this catastrophe.

"Listen," he begged. "Please listen to me. You can't do it. You can't throw your life away."

"Capital punishment was abolished in England years ago."

"But years and years in prison. It amounts to the same thing. You'd be better off dead."

"They'll understand."

"You keep *saying* that," Tom panted. "But think of the disgrace. Think of your wife, your children."

"I have. They were my first concern."

187

"They'll die with the shame."

"Nonsense. I think they'll be rather proud."

"D'you want your children to know they have a murderer for a father?"

"I'm not a murderer. You said so yourself."

"But—"

"Now go home," Jack said. He was tired of the other's importuning. And anyway, this was his own moment. Good or bad, it was his and he didn't want it shared. "Go home."

"No," said Tom, falling back as they turned into the lane between houses. "I won't let you do this."

"You can't stop me."

"Man, you're throwing away everything, and for what?"

"Peace of mind."

"You've had that for thirty years."

"Go home, please."

"No. For God's sake stop walking a minute."

They came out on the common and went into its dimness, Jack striding and Tom hustling at his side as before. Tom gasped, "Won't you stop and listen to me?"

"No. Go home."

About to speak again, Tom held back. An idea was forming. Grappling for it, he walked in silence. Then he stopped abruptly and put his hand to his heart, as if in tribute to the idea. It had come and it was magnificent. Everything could be resolved with the greatest of ease. His own desires, Partridge's conscience, his family's disgrace, everything.

Partridge had turned and was walking back. "Are you all right? Why're you holding your heart?"

"I—I was just a bit breathless."

"Serves you right for running, a man your age. Now go home." Partridge turned and walked on.

188

Tom followed. "One last word," he said, "and then we'll part." From his inside pocket he brought out the length of iron. He gripped one end. "Sure you won't change your mind?"

"Quite sure."

Taking long strides, Tom closed the gap until he was almost walking on the other's heels. He said, "I'll ask you just one more time. Will you forget about the police?"

"No."

Swinging back his arm, Tom made a skipping change of step and brought the iron down with all his strength and all the weight in his body.

Jack Partridge grunted, came to a halt, sagged at the knees. As if being lowered gently by an invisible rope, he sank to the ground, where he rolled over onto his back and lay still.

Tom stood panting for a moment before stepping across and bending down to feel for a sign of life. There was no sign. Jack Partridge was dead.

Tom straightened. Holding in the fork of his hand the middle of the iron he wiped its holding end with his sleeve. He tossed the weapon aside and bent again over the body.

While loading himself with the contents of Partridge's pockets, leaving their linings hanging out like sick tongues, not forgetting to also take the ice pick, which he would drop in a gutter drain, he paused to glance at the head of the dark dead shape and say, "Nothing personal."

After taking Partridge's wristwatch, he was finished. He turned and set off back across the common, striding firmly. He told himself that what he had done was right. It was not a crime but a pleasant pearly grey. It was that word that meant mercy killing. He had saved Jack Partridge from himself and his family from shame. Their mourning would not now be for themselves but for the memory of a fine man, an honoured name. And now he could close the other matter too.

Janet Tree turned over fitfully in bed. Ever since retiring she had been able to do nothing other than sink into a series of dozings. The same thing had happened the night before. She was accustomed to sleeping against the background of comings and goings by her boarders, and, like a city man who spends a night in the country, she found the peace disturbing. Then too, tonight there had been other interruptions. First a soft padding sound which had cut into her sleep the way our city man would be awakened by a faint cock-crow yet not the blast of a train whistle. Later there had been a murmur of voices, still later loud talking outside, an argument that at first seemed to be taking place in the garden.

Now, she was floating once more into a doze when she heard a gentle thud. A door closing? She lifted her head from the pillow to listen. There came another thud. A door again, this time being opened; and this door, she suddenly realized, was that of her parlour.

Leaping from bed she put on a dressing gown. Previously, with her two former boarders in residence, she would have been afraid. With Tom Brady in the house she felt safe, even bold.

She looked into the hall. Her parlour's light was on and its door standing open. She called, "Who's there?"

In the doorway appeared Tom Brady. "Ah," he said cheerfully. "I was just going to use your telephone, Janet."

"Of course, Tom. Help yourself. Sorry I interrupted."

"Glad you did, as a matter of fact. Could you come in here, please? I've got something to say."

Janet went forward. In the parlour Tom was lowering himself to a seat beside the telephone. His face was flushed, his eyes shone. Janet said, "You seem pleased with yourself."

"And why not? I'm about to do something of great importance to us both."

"Both?" she repeated, sitting.

He winked, lifted the receiver and dialled. After a pause he said, "City Police? Good evening. Connect me with the C.I.D., please. It's about murder. What? Yes, young man, I said murder. Yes, I'll wait."

Cuddling the receiver to his neck Tom looked at Janet with a smile. "We are going to be rich and famous, my dear. I'll sell my life story to the newspapers and perhaps you can sell yours too—after we get married, which event will take place in jail, they allow that sort of thing sometimes. How does that sound?"

Blushing, thrilled to her toes, Janet said, "Yes, Tom. It sounds wonderful."

"Excuse me." He returned the instrument to his mouth and began to talk.

Janet listened and looked admiringly, proud of her man. He was so firm, so sure. And the next second she understood everything, the identity of the murderer, why he had not shown up at the bank, what Tom had meant about money and fame, for he was saying:

"That is correct. I want to confess to a murder. I committed it thirty years ago, in London. Her name was Carlotta and I met her first at a dance . . ."